Captured by
My Sister's
Man

Book 2

By

CORNELIA SMITH

Captivated by my sister's man

Copyright © 2015 by Cornelia Smith

All Rights Reserved

www.thebookplug.com

Other Titles
by
Cornelia Smith

Table of Contents

One

RAT TAT TAT TAT TAT TAT TAT
The sound of the assault rifle roared through the village, and panic ripped through Kenya's chest as she was alarmed from her sleep.

"Get up! Get up now, girls!" Her grandma whispered frantically as she urgently shook Kenya and her little sister Sahara.

Kenya's eyes darted around the thatched hut home as her grandma guarded the door. In her grandma's trembling hands, she held a hunting rifle, the only weapon she owned. Seven bullets were all she had left from the weeks of hunting.

"Grandma, what are you doing? You don't know how to shoot that!" Kenya quickly snatched the rifle from her grandmother. Since her brother's death, she had been the only one hunting for the family. She took over her brother's responsibilities and became the man of the family.

"Kenya, I can't lose you. We can't lose you." Kenya eyed Grandma Eartha and then her little sister and three younger cousins.

"Sahara, I'm depending on you to take care of this family, and whatever you do, don't quit playing chess. It's our way out of here." Tears streamed from Sahara's eyes and down her cheeks. Just the thought of losing Kenya turned her stomach.

"Go hide!" Stiff as mannequins, no one moved; instead, they all stared at Kenya with their wet eyes.

"Go hide now, dammit!" Hesitant, everyone but Kenya went and found cover. As much as she wanted to run and hide with her family, Kenya knew she had to stand her ground. With only seven bullets in the rifle, Kenya knew she was about to fight an unmatched battle - an unwinnable war. Her impending death was near, but she silently prayed that her actions would be enough to spare her family. She squared her shoulders like her father had once taught her before being killed to appear strong, but she was afraid, and her fear was like poison that spread to her heart. She was sick with silent grief as she anticipated the torture to come.

"Kenya, what do you see?" Grandma Eartha yelled in confusion, eyes wide and heart rattled, as gunshots rang out loudly. The sound of rowdy men grew increasingly louder as the violence grew near. Their whoops and hollers were barbaric as they screamed out their hateful chants, full of pure adrenaline, as they announced their presence.

"Shit, it's worse than I thought. It's Rasheed and his gang." Kenya revealed.

"No, Kenya! You must hide. You know his obsession with you." Grandma Eartha screamed out as she darted towards the door.

"No! No! You can't go out there. They will kill you!" Eartha said as she grabbed her granddaughter's trembling hand.

"It's the very reason I must go, Grandma. It's me he wants, and whether I go out there or stay in here, he's going to get me. At least this way, he'll only get me, not the people I love."

"They will hurt you!" Sahara screamed out. Eartha cried as the thought of her brave granddaughter facing the monster, Rasheed, and his heartless gang alone caused her to tremble.

"Enough, everybody. That's enough! I'm going to handle this myself. It's the only way. We must keep this family together. It was all momma wanted." Kenya kissed her grandmother on the cheek. Her terror crippled her as pools of tears formed, and the dreams of tomorrow washed away in streams that flowed down her cheeks.

"But grandma?" Sahara cried out with big, pleading eyes.

"She's in God's hands now, Sahara. It is up to a higher power to keep her safe. It is my responsibility to keep you three safe." Grandma Eartha took Sahara by the hand and shoved her into the closet.

"They're getting closer," Kenya said as her eyes darted toward the door. She gripped the gun so tightly that the palms of her dark hands lost all color, and her fingers throbbed. Her breath was short, shallow. She was suffocating in silent affliction as she stared at the door. Her gut told her that this would be the last time she would ever be in the presence of her family. Kenya fought the emotion that threatened to spill from her eyes, and her pride remained intact. She kept her tears at bay and prepared to fight her life to save her family. *It was the only way*, she told herself.

"I love you," Sahara whispered. She looked into her big sister's eyes as she stared into Kenya's face. In her eyes, she saw undeniable grief. Even at the tender age of nine, she recognized her sadness, and her soul bled as her heart became heavy with uncertainty. The madness surrounding her filled her with anxiety, and she could hear her pulse racing as her heart galloped with intensity. She could see Kenya mourning her very own death before it even occurred.

"Sister?" Sahara said as a lump filled her throat.

"You got this," she murmured as Kenya kneeled to kiss her. Her lips were wet and trembling, and though kissing was something the sisters did every day, Sahara knew this might be the last kiss she would ever receive from her sister, so she cherished it. She closed her eyes and locked the brief yet intimate moment into her memory. When Sahara finally looked up, she saw Kenya's back as she headed back over to the door.

"Back in the closet now... hurry!" Kenya whispered. For what seemed like forever, they waited... waited for death in silence while their eyes focused on the rickety door that separated safety from destruction.

3

Finally, after thirty long seconds, Rasheed's gang invaded Kenya's home mercilessly, kicking in the door, and without thinking, Kenya let loose the power from her rifle. Hitting the first man that came through the door. She aimed her father's old rusty gun and fired away. The cadence of the gun matched the pace of Kenya's heart. She wanted to close her eyes but was too afraid to blink. One man after another. Kenya shot seven men with her seven bullets. Their blood-covered bodies lay stiff in her eating area.

"You bitch! You killed my fuckin brother." One gang member cried out, dropping to his knees to comfort his dying sibling.

"Oh, you're going to die slow, bitch!" Another gang member added. Kenya looked into the gang member's eyes, and she knew he wasn't lying. She was going to die slowly. The ruthlessness that she saw caused her fingertips to grow ice cold. She was staring into an empty shell, a dark soul whose intention was bloodshed. As he circled her like a predator stalking his prey, her beats increased.

"God, forgive me as I have sinned..." Kenya whispered her prayer as the gang member continued to circle her with an amused smile on his face. He stepped behind her and gripped her neck, applying pressure as he bent her over.

"You coward!" Kenya screamed out. The gang member ripped the thin fabric of Kenya's skirt and forced her against the wall as he roughly spread her legs. The wretched scent of his breath filled her nostrils as she screamed in protest.

"Don't touch me, you filthy animal!" He ignored her cry and thrust his fingers into her vagina.

"Enough!" a voice bellowed from behind the mob of men who watched. Trembling, Sahara and the girls clung to each other, arms intertwined desperately as if they had the strength to stay connected that way forever. They watched in trepidation as the men parted and Rasheed stepped forward. The thud of his heavy combat boots beat the dirt floor, resounding like an African drum, providing the soundtrack to the massacre he had brought upon the village.

"Go rally the others. Make sure every hut has been searched. Take every girl you see," Rasheed ordered without ever taking his eyes off the prize.

"Well, isn't this too good to be true? She's beautiful, and she knows how to kill." Rasheed grizzly laugh haunted Kenya.

"Didn't I tell you, you would mine?" Kenya resisted as Rasheed dragged her to the door.

"You should've just come when I asked you to." Kenya's tiny fists did little to stop Rasheed from imposing his will. Quickly, he tossed her into the jeep, and his driver drove off. The rest of the gang members followed behind in their identical jeeps. Kenya cried, but weirdly, they were tears of joy. Her plan had worked; she had kept her family safe.

Kenya rode in the jeep bed and watched five other jeeps follow them up the mountains where Rasheed resided. She paid close attention to her surroundings and kept a map of where she was going. The altitude got higher as the jeeps wrapped around the mountain that sat in the middle of the jungle. Rasheed's estate sat at the top, and what looked like a small house soon proved to be a large mansion once they got closer to it. Kenya allowed the beautiful trees and fresh air to calm her nerves. There was something about Africa's fresh air that soothed her.

The smell of rain always filled the air, even though it hadn't rained in months in Sierra Leone. The cool, damp air was refreshing, and the deeper they got, the more exotic and beautiful it became. The beautiful trees and exotic birds put Kenya in deep thought, and before she knew it, they had reached the top of the mountain where the large Mediterranean home sat. Young militants were scattered everywhere on guard protecting their queen. As soon as they pulled up, the jeep stopped in front of the home, and Rasheed and his driver got out.

"Come on!" Rasheed yelled out to Kenya. Shooters paced the upper wraparound porch. Some were even on the roof. Kenya paid close attention to the detail. She was going to try to escape. She followed Rasheed toward the house, and every time Rasheed passed a militant, they saluted him by putting their hand to their forehead. Once they entered the house, the refreshing central air hit their bodies like the cool breeze from an ocean. Although their country was somewhat less advanced than the U.S., the inside of Rasheed's home wasn't. Gold life-sized lion sculptures sat by the doorway, and marble floors set the tone for the extravagant home.

The high cathedral ceiling had a diamond chandelier hanging eight feet down to add flair. It was simply amazing.

"Welcome to your new home," Rasheed said as he gently put his hand on Kenya's shoulder. She aggressively jerked away.

"Don't be like that. I'm being nice. I'm giving you a chance to meet the queen."

"London! Honey, I have a surprise for you."

Two

"London!" Rasheed yelled as he looked up the grand staircase. The opulent double stairs were the room's centerpiece as they met at a balcony at the top. Moments later, all eyes were on the second floor when a butterscotch beauty queen appeared. Her flawless, smooth skin, thick, bursting lips, and slim body were breathtaking. Kenya looked up in awe as she admired her slim body and beauty. She wore matte red lipstick, which matched her silky blonde hair. She wore a white silk robe that didn't do much to hide her body. Her legs were long and toned as if she was a professional athlete. Her ass was also toned and very petite.

London looked down onto the main floor, and when she laid eyes on Kenya, she immediately felt sympathy for her.

"Why are you calling out my name like that?" London snapped at Rasheed.

"I want you to bathe her and give her something to wear," Rasheed yelled out to London back as she walked away.

"Go on, follow her," Rasheed said to Kenya.

.... *THREE HOURS LATER*

"You two are all the dream I need," Rasheed said as he circled the black beauty Kenya. Her dark chocolate skin and thick full lips made her desirable. She was perfect in every way, young, thick, and untouched.

"Your father was right to keep you away from me. That's why I had to eliminate him." London watched Rasheed fiend for Kenya like a dog in heat. He was worse than disgusting in her book.

"You killed my daddy, you bastard." Kenya's sobbing weakened London's heart. She could barely watch, but she knew things would get worse for Kenya if she left the room.

"I had to. It was the only way I could have you all to myself. You see, I have craved you for a long time, and I wasn't going to let know that overprotective warrior get in my way." Kenya dropped down to her knees and broke into tears.

"If you touch her, you raggedy piece of shit. You can never have me again." London knew the consequences of talking to Rasheed in any way, but she was willing to sacrifice for Kenya. She was only a baby. No sixteen-year-old should have to suffer the Rasheed effect.

"How dare you disrespect me in front of our company?" Quickly, Rasheed charged at London, but she didn't budge. He was so close to her she could lick his face.

"Don't you ever talk to me that way in my house!" His heavy tone and devilish eyes did nothing to London. She was like a walking dead-zombie. There was nothing Rasheed could do to her that he hadn't already done.

"I mean it, Rasheed. You cannot have us both. Period. So, choose?" London's calm but demanding tone always got under Rasheed's skin. It was like she knew just the right buttons to press to piss him off. Roughly, he gripped her neck and slung her onto the king-size bed. Kenya jumped up from the floor, in a position to jump on Rasheed's back. She was ready to risk her life for London; after all, she was only in trouble with Rasheed for standing up for her. Just as Kenya took her first step, London shook her head *no*. She knew they were outnumbered and had seen Rasheed at his worst. He could be worse than horrible.

"So, I have to choose?" Rasheed hovered like a rabid dog as he ripped London's robe from her body. His penis rose in sexual heat as his eyes stalked her body.

"I choose you! And you better make it worth my time, or I'm going to give miss thing over there something to remember." The sweat that dripped from his thick brow felt like acid on London's breast.

"You better not take your eyes off me, or all bets are off!" Rasheed turned back to yell at Kenya as he entered London, defiling her womanhood, filling every hole of her body with shame as he thrust wildly.

Kenya whimpered loudly as she watched the rape helplessly. Her young body was paralyzed in agony as she witnessed the unspeakable act of sin. She watched blankly as Rasheed pounded on London like she was an African drum. She screamed until she couldn't anymore, then whimpered until her whimpers became moans. It was as if she was holding on to life by a strand. When the moans stopped, Kenya knew London's soul had left her body. Rasheed's body jerked like a stick-shift Honda and poured his heirs into London right after.

"You're going to give me a son. I can feel it." he groaned out before his body dropped dead onto London's.

####

Slowly, London put her hands under her head and laid back all the way so the water filled her ears. But she could still hear Kenya ramble on about her family from under the water. London was tired, and her body was sore. She just wanted to rest and put the horrific experience behind her. After thirty minutes, the water was still a little warm, and London planned to stay in until the water grew cold.

"So, enough about me," Kenya said as she softly rubbed the sponge up and down London's neck and shoulders.

"Where are you from, and how long have you been in Sierra Leone?"

"Sierra Leone?" Water splashed Kenya's face as London lifted from under the water.

"Yes, you mean to tell me you didn't know where you were?" Shameful, London nodded her head. It was true for five years; Rasheed kept their location a secret. London knew she was in Africa from the small villages and jungles, but no one would tell her what part of Africa, on Rasheed's orders.

"Listen, I think I know my way back out of here. I'm going to make a run for it. Are you coming?" Slowly, London slid her body back into the warm water. Kenya was talking nonsense.

"You'll never make it. It's nothing but trees out there." London muttered.

"I know my way through the jungle. It was a short thirty to forty- five minutes drive. We will not have that far to run." Silently, London thought. *Lions, snakes, monkeys, run forty-five minutes with angry militant men after us. Yeah, I'll pass.*

"Thank you for the sponge bath, but if you don't mind, I'll like to be left alone." With glistening eyes, Kenya stared directly through London's nude body. She couldn't understand why she wouldn't even try to make a run for it.

"Don't you have some family you want to get home to?" Kenya softly spoke with a lump in her throat. She waited for a response, but London never gave her one. Instead, she lay in the tub with her eyes closed, humming Stevie Wonder's *Happy Birthday* song.

Three

"**H**appy birthday to you, happy birthday to you." Paris sang out to baby Kash in between the wet kisses she plotted on his cheeks.

"Mom, stop; you're embarrassing me." Screaming swarms of children ran through the house as bubbles floated in the air and balloons drifted around aimlessly on the floor among the discarded wrapping paper.

"Are you too big to kiss me now?" Again, Paris left another little wet mark, a shallow pool of saliva on baby Kash's cheek.

"Momma, not right now."

"Okay, okay! Are you ready to open your presents?" A stack of unopened presents stood in the corner of the room, wrapped in shiny wrapping paper. A silk bow had been carefully tied around each parcel.

"Baby, let's feed the kids first. We don't want to let the food get cold." Hungry children loomed over the table, which was filled with food. They grabbed at sandwiches and filled their mouths with sweets.

"Wait, wait. Let's make a line, kids!" Not one of the kids listened to Paris. Like a chicken with its head cut off, Paris ran after the kids, attempting to get an order. After five years, she still felt like a new parent. Kash, on the other hand, had parenting down the pack.

"One. Two. Three..." Before Kash reached five, all the kids stood at attention. Breathing over the food like little puppies, patiently, they waited for instructions. A huge cake covered in thick red and blue icing and decorated with spider man gadgets sat in the middle of the table, surrounded by brightly colored bowls that were filled with food.

"What would you like - hot dog or chicken?" Paris assumed her position and made the kids' plates.

"Oooh...!" The kids sang in unison. A jug of brightly colored juice had been knocked over, forming a puddle on the floor.

"You knocked Kash juice down, Rodrick." One little boy screamed out.

"I didn't mean to...!" Tears streamed down Rodrick's face as he screamed until he caught Paris's attention.

"Listen. Listen. It's okay. Don't cry." Gently, Paris rubbed Rodrick's back to soothe his crying, but he only got louder. Easily, he had pushed Paris overboard. She was already fragile. She missed her sister more each birthday, and his loud yelling broke her.

Her tears burst forth like water from a dam; they spilled down her face. She could feel the muscles of her chin tremble like a small child, so she looked toward the window, trying to avoid eye contact with anyone. There is static in her head once more, the side effect of this constant fear that London will never get to see her baby boy grow up. For years Paris has lived with this constant stress. She let go of Rodrick and quickly dashed to the nearest bathroom, which was in the hall next to the guest bedroom.

The chaotic room suddenly became still. All eyes were on Paris's absence. The kids were confused, but the adults sort of knew what was going on.

"Give me a minute, Omari." Kash dashed down the hall before Dr. Omari could respond.

"Baby, open the door." Softly, Paris pressed her head against the door. It shook and trembled as Kash pounded on it. Her eyes dripped with tears. Her walls, the walls that held her up and made her strong, just... collapsed. The salty drops that fail from her chin drenched her shirt.

"I'm okay, Kash." She screeched out with a thump in her throat. She was everything, but okay. Paris couldn't stop trembling. *She thought, "Why can't I stop crying* as the pain came in waves, minutes of sobbing broken apart by short pauses for recovery breaths.

"Baby, you're not okay. Just let me hold you."

"Kash, please... Just finish the party for me. Baby Kash needs you more right now." Hesitantly, Kash returned to the party.

"Who wants cake?" he screamed into the crowd of kids.

"Meeeee!" The kids sang in unison, running full speed towards the cake table.

"We can take care of it, Kash." Gently, Omari's wife, Jordan, took the cake knife from Kash's hand. He was in no mood to cut the cake. It was obvious that Paris's loud whimpering from the back of the house was eating at his nerves. Kash felt helpless. He had run out of ways to soothe his wife's pain.

"Thank you," Kash muttered, taking Jordan up on her offer. He knew it was wrong for both Baby Kash's parents to walk out on his big day, but he suddenly needed air and a moment to vent himself. The crowd of mothers watched as Kash fought back the tears. He respectfully excused himself, and as soon as he reached the back porch, he yelled out, "Fuck!" hitting the back of the house so hard that he instantly regretted it as his hand exploded with pain. "Fuck! Fuck! Fuck!" he shouted, half out of pain and half out of anger. He just wanted his life back.

"Brother, I can help?" Omari's voice startled Kash. Slowly, he turned around, trying his best to hide his true frustrations.

"We'll be fine, man. It just gets harder around these times. Plus, the private investigator that we hired was killed a few weeks back, so Paris has lost hope again." Omari listened attentively to Kash as he attempted not to notice his tears.

"It's like we take one step and pull back three. We know London is alive. Well, at least she was two months ago. And we know she's in Africa, held captive with some monster. Only, we don't know the real name of the monster or where in Africa. Shit, man Africa is big as hell. She could be damn where." Omari crept up behind Kash as his back was turned, facing their beautiful yard to pat him on the back.

"Brother, I'm going to West Africa in a couple of days. I know Africa, like you know *basketball*. It's my home." Omari's accent wasn't as heavy as a normal African's, but his English wasn't perfect. He didn't always stress certain words enough, but his dedication to improving his speech made it impossible not to forgive him for those minor shortcomings, such as occasionally stumbling over the word basketball.

"You're going to West Africa?" Kash lifted from the banister like he saw the light.

"Yes, I have some missionary work to do down there, and I can put my ear in the street and see what I can find out."

"Man, you would do that?" Kash flashed his pearly white teeth for the time all day.

"Yes, that's not a problem."

"Thank you, Omari. If you don't mind, let's keep this between you and me. I don't want to get Paris's hopes all up. Plus, if she finds out you're going to South Africa, she might just invite herself." Together the two men laughed as they made their way back into the house. As they reached the living area, their laughs faded away. They were surprised to see Paris had returned to the party. She thanked the mothers for coming as she handed them candy bags on their way out the door.

Four

Kenya woke up like a bucket of water was poured onto her. No sleepiness, no slow warming up. Within seconds of realizing she was conscious, she was back on her feet, eyes wide, dreams not just forgotten but obliterated. She had fallen asleep in the jungle after hours of running, and she was only halfway to her destination. The woods were simply too dark to see, black tree trunks against an almost black backdrop didn't make for much of a vision, but she couldn't afford to stay still.

She had to keep running. Kenya had rather take on the horrors of the jungle than be Rasheed's sex slave for the rest of her life. She ran like she was forest dashing through the dark. The jungle heat and humidity pressed in on her skin, making sweat pointless. The sounds of the insects, the birds, and the larger animals created a symphony of nature calling her deeper. The leaves brushed up against her, and her feet sprung up with each step. The air tasted both sweet and fresh, like flowers blooming on her tongue.

So far, she had been lucky. She hadn't been attacked, of course, by leeches and mosquitoes and stinging ants.

But the more dangerous animals, like the snakes and scorpions, had left her alone. The rivers she had crossed had been free of the real spooky animals. She had survived some of the jungle's most dangerous big shots.

Low on breath, she stopped to catch a break. Trees tall as cathedrals surrounded Kenya, and suddenly she spotted a strange green light-almost holy-shimmer through the vast canopy of leaves.

"Good. The Kantu village," she muttered between breaths before taking off full speed, chasing the light. Eye on the prize destination, Kenya didn't bother looking back or around for that matter, only straight ahead. She was weak, hungry, thirsty, and needed shelter. She was so focused she failed to notice the armed men hiding behind the tall trees. Her captivity was simpler than she had imagined it to be. In her head, she saw herself putting up a fight—punching, kicking, biting, and spitting but she didn't get a chance to do either. With one hit to the head, she was out.

She drifted into consciousness. And then back out. The world was a blur, and random images seemed to float aimlessly around in the pool of her thoughts. A kick on her shoulder momentarily brought her back to the outside world, but she was once again lost after a second. She could feel somebody looking at her, staring her dead in the eye, but she couldn't keep focus. The whole world simply felt low resolution, a bad quality movie. Confusion blossomed in her heart, and she knew that, eventually, she would need to wake up. To stare reality in the face.

But for the moment, she laid down her heavy head and retreated into wallowing blackness.

####

Kenya's head jolted upward, letting her know she was unconscious. The light of late morning shone into her slowly opening eyes, and she attempted to bring her hand to guard them, but she quickly discovered they were tied behind her back to a chair. Everything about her felt heavy, from her arms to her feet. She let her head loll from one side to the other, eyes closing one more time as she enjoyed the brief darkness.

"Well, hello, sleeping beauty?" Rasheed stepped closer to Kenya, grinning freakishly. Her eyes rushed about, scanning the room, and there helpless, she spotted London's naked body, each of her limbs bound to a bedpost. A tight handkerchief muffled her mouth while her eyes darted around the bedroom.

"What have you done to her?" Kenya screamed out.

"You know, I think the better question is what I'm going to do to her? I couldn't dare let you miss the show."

"What are you going to do to her? She didn't do anything; it was me who tried to run away! Punish me." Rasheed closed his eyes and slightly grinned as if he was envisioning his sweetest memory. He took his time before speaking, wanting to be as accurate and vivid as humanly possible.

"First, I'm going to torture her for hours... slowly, I want her to feel death without experiencing it. It will be perfect. So painful. Then, once she has learned her lesson." Quickly, Kenya interrupted and screamed, "But she didn't do anything; it was me!"

"But she did, you see. She allowed you to disrespect me. Had I handled you my way, you would've never run. So, since you are her responsibility, she must pay for your mistakes." Slowly, tears dripped from Kenya's smokey grey eyes. She hated that London was paying for her behavior.

"Please, Rasheed!" Kenya cried out.

"Now, that's what I'm talking about. Beg... Beg...!" Rasheed was a man of power with a sick obsession for women begging him. Kenya noticed the slight erection that showed through Rasheed's slacks. It was at that moment that Kenya realized what her begging did to Rasheed.

"You're a sick asshole. Let me loose, and I'll kick your ass!" Rasheed ignored little Kenya and circled London's body like she was prey. He had purposely left London tied up for hours to torture her more. He knew It was the waiting that drove her insane. London felt as though she was sitting on death row. The actual time spent anticipating the horrific event was punishment itself. Rasheed understood this, and it gave him extreme satisfaction.

"The next time you think about leaving me, I want you to think of my beautiful, who has been so nice to you. I want you to think about how she benefits from your absence." Rasheed walked over to his closet and pulled out a long leather belt. He anticipated this moment for hours, and it literally made his dick hard thinking about what he was about to do. He walked over to London while grinning and slowly popped the belt. London's muffled screams didn't affect Rasheed at all as he thought about the pain he was about to inflict.

"If you close your eyes once or turn your head an inch. I will piss all over her and maybe even shit." He turned to say to Kenya before he began to strike London with all his might. He hit her all over her body, leaving red marks with each lashing. Rasheed struck her repeatedly, and this was only the beginning. He was determined to make her suffer in the worst way. After beating her until he had no more strength, he began performing oral sex on London, and this lasted for three hours straight while she was still bound, and there was nothing pleasurable about his touch. He sucked and nibbled and licked on her roughly.

Sucking on her until she was raw. He was absolutely obsessed with London and even more in love with Kenya watching his obsession. Rasheed was sweating to the point of exhaustion as he pleased himself; all the while, he was torturing London and Kenya at once. By now, London could sob no more. She had cried her eyes out and was basically numb to the annoyance. She stared blankly into space as Rasheed rose and maneuvered himself into a missionary position over London. He entered her treasure box and slowly stroked her as he kissed her forehead passionately.

"I promised you I would never fuck her, and I haven't. You see, I'm not that bad of a monster." Rasheed began to enjoy sex with London; as he looked down at her, it was as if she wasn't even there. Kenya had given up on screaming; instead, she just prayed aloud. She prayed and began to talk to God from the time Rasheed began his torture. Meanwhile, London didn't even blink as her mind drifted to her one true love...Gunner.

As Rasheed began to pound away, London got lost in his gaze as she pictured his face as Gunner's staring into hers. Once upon of time, he would have burst down the door to save her from the torture she was enduring, but he was no longer around to protect her. Still, the thought of him brought her mental relief.

Rasheed felt a climax approaching as he began to pump feverishly and aggressively. Sweat dripped from his forehead and onto London's naked body as a river of semen shot inside of her. Rasheed smiled and looked down at London. He saw a single tear slide down her cheek, but the blank stare she wore never left her face. He chuckled at her pain, and in response, she spat into his face, disrespecting his power. He slid out of her and stood up, leaving the saliva to drip from his face.

"I just love your courage," Rasheed said before zipping his pants.

"Go make yourself useful and give her a sponge bath." Rasheed looked at Kenya with disgust while untying her from the chair.

Five

Paris propped up the girls in a Miracle C-cup, checked the smooth, waxed bikini line in her thong, and released her shoulder-length hair from a barrette, proud she'd made an appointment at True Groovy to iron out her impressive mane of curls earlier in the day. Just as she slipped on her dress, baby Kash called from the door, "Mommy, you smell good." As she turned, she stopped mid-smile at the sight of baby Kash perched atop Kash's shoulders.

"Yeah, MILF, I haven't seen you this beautiful since—well, you're always beautiful. Are you trying to make me jealous?" Kash asked, hoping to provoke a smile. "You don't have a secret admirer behind their bars, do you?" Kash was careful not to offend Paris. He needed to get back in her corner, back into her accommodating thighs.

"I don't want no man that's locked down in the penitentiary. I hate even going. Just the smell of that place creeps me out. But I want to look that Gunner in his eyes while I talk to him. That a..." Quick, Paris remembered baby Kash was present and cut her sentence short.

"May I have five minutes to get dressed? Please." Kash walked out the door with baby Kash blowing kisses at Paris. She rolled her eyes at Kash's back. Ten years of unconditional, unfiltered love. *Ten years of supporting him through his career, and he won't even try to stop cheating.* She shook her head in disgust as her mind drifted back two weeks.

That Wednesday, Kash ambled into the living room, parked himself on the sectional, turned on the game, and flickered through the newspaper like he and she weren't supposed to be out on a date. He recited his routine lies – "Work kept him longer than he expected," "he ate at the house." He grabbed a Corona from the fridge and then took a good look at Paris, all dressed up.

"Where are you going?" He had the nerve to ask.

"Well, I was going out with my husband, but I guess nowhere." She glared at him with anger in her eyes as he paced back and forth in the living room, his Prada's leaving small tracks in the carpet.

"I'm sorry, baby, I got caught up at work, and it totally slipped my mind."

"I always seem to slip your mind." She shouted. Paris counted the many times she had been put last on Kash's list.

"Forget it, Kash," is how she moved on from every problem she had with Kash. She wished like hell she had the type of courage London was blessed with. If she did, she would have told Kash off. She'd tell him that she knew he was cheating, and she would threaten to leave him for doing so.

Shaking off the bullshit, Paris grabbed her keys and stormed down the stairs past the boys. "Bye, you two. I'll call as soon as I can."

Rushing to the prison, she weaved in and out of traffic on I-75; she tailed Atlanta police, riding full speed, caring less about a ticket. She was pushing for time, and she'd be dammed if she missed visitation. Just as she approached her exit, Kash called.

"Is everything okay, baby?" Paris knew exactly why Kash was calling, but she played the dixie wife so well that she sometimes almost fooled herself.

"Yes, but something came up at work, so I'm going to take little Kash to your mother's house. You can pick him up from there." Paris knew the call was coming. Kash could never just spend a day with little Kash without her present. He'd rather run around with his little side thang, who he thought Paris knew nothing about.

"I really didn't want Kash over there this week. Momma needs a break." Paris sighed softly, but she kept her frustration in control. She never wanted to upset Kash. She hated it when they argued.

"No, I squared it away with her, and she said it's fine." Without thinking, Paris snapped.

"Yes, of course she did, Kash. She's never going to tell us no, even if she needs a break." By the end of her sentence, Paris had noticed her tone and quickly tried to fix it before it led to her and Kash screaming at one another.

"Okay, I'll call her," she said rapidly before Kash could respond to her outburst.

"Okay, call me when you make it back home." If Kash could see the way Paris rolled her eyes as she looked down at her iPhone, he would know how pissed she was, but he knew of no frustration because Paris sounded as jolly as a Christmas commercial. "Okay, baby, I'll call you as soon as I'm back. I shouldn't be that long." What she really wanted to say was, *I'm not coming back. I'm going to a hotel for the weekend for some time, and I'm not answering my phone.*

"Okay, talk to you soon."

"Okay, love you, bye." Racing to a parking spot in the crowded parking lot, Paris didn't bother to put her phone back into her purse until the car was parked. The Latina chic with the blonde hair talked major shit to Paris for stealing her spot, but Paris couldn't hear what she was saying because both her windows were rolled up.

"Yeah. Yeah. Get over it; it's just a parking spot." Paris mumbled as she watched the Latina continue with her rant.

####

The sound of Paris tapping her heel echoed throughout the waiting room. Her leg shook like a branch on a tree. Nervously, she waited for her name to be called. She had been forced to sit next to the feisty Latina from the parking lot. It was the only seat left in the crowded room. Scuffling through her purse for some gum, Paris didn't bother rushing to the door when the guard called for Gunner's visitors, but she was surprised to see that the Latina chic quickly bounced up from her seat at the sound of Gunner's name. Curious, Paris allowed her to lead the way.

All eyes set on the Latina's beauty. Most did not pay attention to her beauty but rather her shape. She was built like a black woman. Round ass and thick thighs never looked so good on a woman. With black hair of wool and her head held high, she waltzed on with an effortless saunter. The clicking of her heels added to the already noisy waiting room. Her eyes scanned the room with a devilish stare. When Paris and the Latina met eyes, they both rolled them like mean girls in high school.

Stunned like a deer in headlights, Gunner was speechless when he saw both Cardi and Paris walk into the room. Two beauties at once would usually be a jailbird's dream, but not for Gunner. He watched Paris blankly as she made her way towards his table. Paris wasn't beautiful in the Instagram-model-popping way, with no huge ass or long weave. She was shorter than the average supermodel, and her natural hair was only shoulder length, but in her ordinariness, she was stunning. Something radiated from within that rendered her irresistible to both genders. Men desired her, and women courted her friendship.

"So, who is she, Gunner?" she snapped before taking a seat at the table, pointing to Cardi.

"Oh, London, don't act like you don't know who I am." Cardi's twenty-six-inch weave swung from side to side as she rolled her neck and pointed her finger at Paris.

"Anyway, I thought you said she was gone, Gunner." Stuck, Gunner stuttered... "Um...thisssss... is nottt."

"I'm not London, bitch!" Paris's emotions were not easily hidden on her innocent face. Her pain was evident in the crease of her lovely brow and the down-curve of her full lips. But her eyes, her eyes showed her soul. They were a deep pool of restless gold, an ocean of hopeless grief.

"How dare you just move on and forget my sister when you are the fucking reason she's missing in the first place." As Gunner looked into Paris's eyes, he knew he had fucked up. It was as if London was staring him down herself.

"Sister?"

"Yes, bitch! Sister. We're twins." Cardi couldn't believe her ears, but it had all made sense now. London would have popped off on Cardi in the parking lot quick. They couldn't stand each other, and she wasn't one to bite her tongue or walk away from a confrontation so easily as Paris did.

"It's not what you think," Gunner finally drummed up the courage to say.

"What I think is, you've moved on with your life and forgot about my sister."

"How could I ever forget about London? Think about what you are saying! It's just not too much I can do from in here." Paris wasn't hearing it; she shook her head. Gunner's words weren't good enough.

"My sister is somewhere fighting for her life because of you, and this is all you have to say. She's fighting for her life while you're in here playing pimp daddy." Badly, Gunner wanted to explain to Paris how messing with Cardi benefited him, but he couldn't do that without offending Cardi.

"Bitch, who is he pimping?" Cardi snapped.

"If you knew what was good for you bitch, you'll shut the fuck up!" It was at that moment Cardi realized Paris had a gangster in her blood. She smacked her teeth and rolled her eyes but didn't utter another word.

"Paris?" Paris bountiful breast bounced up and down in her fitted blouse as she jumped up from the table. Before walking off, she turned around to face Gunner one last time.

"Paris, what?" She snapped

"Don't leave like this." Gunner pleaded.

"Is there any information you can give me that can help me find my sister?"

"I don't have nothing right..."

"Yes or No, Gunner?" Paris's voice echoed throughout the room.

"No..." he answered shamefully, and before he knew it, a mouth full of Paris's saliva slapped him in his face.

"That's exactly what I thought." Gunner waved the guard off Paris without a second thought. He didn't want her to catch any trouble on his account. After all, he felt he deserved every ounce of her disrespect.

####

"Look, man, I know I was supposed to pay you today, but my people didn't come through, so I'm going to have to get that little bit after I make these moves." Gunner stared blankly at the picture of London hanging on the wall above his bunk. He had let her down, and the guilt was eating away at his gut. He was all she had in life. How could he fail her so miserably? He thought.

"First of all, you not going to tell me what you going to do when it comes down to my money." Gunner finally turned away from London to face the problem head-on. This is the first time Rock gets to see his eyes. They're dark, bloodshot, and filled with anger.

"Man, look. I can only do what I can do. I can't stress about something that's out of my control. Being in this mother-fucka is stressful enough. Besides, it's not like I'm saying I'm not going to give it to you. You just have to wait to get the money." It takes Gunner a while before he responds. Rock stands in front of him with his arms crossed, ready for whatever. Once, Gunner gets up on his feet and says, "I got to do what, again? Run that by me one more time." Repeatedly, Gunner poked Rock's shoulder with his pointer finger. Aggressively, Rock shoved his hand away from him.

"Man, listen, Gunner. If you want to go there, we can go there. But I'm going to give you your damn money." in that frozen second between standoff and fighting, their eyes flicked at one another. Their faces were unreadable, no fear, no invitational smirk. Gunner had enough frustration built up to fight ten rounds, and that was what he intended to do. Striking the first blow, Gunner showed no mercy. He was full of anger.

"Aight, Gunner man. Damn! Chill, aight." A sudden gush of pain jolted throughout Rock's body. His stomach ached, his arms lost tension, and his legs weakened. Quickly, Gunner had gotten the best of him. His tongue was soaked in the taste of blood. Just as Gunner positioned Rock's head so he could snap his neck, Gunner's roommate jumped in to break it up.

"Aight, chill, Gunner. Chill man. Shit going to be aight, dog." It was like Chad's words waken Gunner from a bad dream. He shook his head and snapped out of the bad spell. Once Rock was free, he quickly left the room but not without saying to Gunner one last time, "I got you, man. I'm going to pay you your money."

Six

The beams of the morning light crept through the blinds of the hotel room. London slowly opened her eyes and felt the weight of a body on her breast. She looked down to see Rasheed peacefully sleeping on her. He had crept into bed late at night and climbed on top of her. He didn't even bother rolling over when he was done doing his business. He just slept where he failed. London frowned with disgust as she looked down at the sleeping beast. Then suddenly, a light bulb flicked on in her head, and her frown easily turned into a smile.

She had easily forgotten how manipulative she was and how treacherous she could be. It was time she started using what she got to get what she wanted. *That's right, London, put your feelings away and hustle hat on,* she thought as she stared down at Rasheed snoring away. She took a deep breath and closed her eyes. Painful images of Rasheed torturing her appeared in her mind. She hated him so much. Tears formed in her eyes, and a single drop cascaded down her cheek. The wound was still fresh, and London could feel the pain physically as if it was still happening.

London slid from underneath Rasheed and stood up. Rasheed was sound asleep, snoring like a grizzly bear in Paris. London could very much kill him right now while he slept if she wanted to. Only it wouldn't guarantee her a way home. The whole of Africa would be hunting for her head. She wiped her tears away and headed toward the shower. She only had a few hours to herself before Rasheed woke up, and she'd rather take her showers while he was asleep so he wouldn't get the bright idea to join her.

London made her way over to the beautiful glass shower and stepped in, letting the hot water cascade down her sore body. At that point, more tears began to flow freely as the burden of not having anybody in her corner sunk in. Paris was her only family, and Gunner was her protector; now that she had neither, she felt alone in the world. Kenya was there, but she was nothing like family, like blood. "Paris," London cried out as she softly banged on the wall, trying to release the pain that was building from within. She wanted her old life back. She missed her family.

After ten minutes, London eventually regained her composure and turned off the water. She grabbed a towel and wrapped it around her dripping body as she headed out of the bathroom. Her heart dropped when she looked at the bed. There was no one there. Rasheed had left. She panicked. With Rasheed gone, so was her chance of getting cash from him while he was in a good mood. She needed to pay the doctor for her monthly routine birth control pills before he left the country on his trip. Whenever she was in the dark house with Rasheed, he would take all her cash as punishment.

"Fuck!" she yelled, biting down on her bottom lip. She ran to the large windows and looked out and saw that his car was no longer parked out front. "Shit," she murmured. She plopped down on the bed and shook her head in defeat. Life had continued to fuck her raw without a condom. Her luck had gone from bad to worse in the blink of an eye. If she missed the doctor, she would have no one to get birth control from. And the last thing she needed was a baby by Rasheed. It would be no way possible she could run away from him then. He would hold on to her for dear life.

Hearing someone slowly opening the door, London quickly hugged her waist and tightened her robe around her waist. Her eyes fixated on the door. "Who's there?" she mumbled.

28

"It's me, baby; who you thought it was?" Rasheed said as he closed the door behind him.

"Oh, I didn't know where you were. I didn't see your car parked outside." While London talked, Rasheed laid out a beautiful black velvet cloth across the bed. With her mouth drooped open, London was speechless. He saw the shock registered on her face before she could hide it. A small smile played on his lips.

"Do you like them?" he asked. At first glance, London would have sworn it was chunks of clear glass; given the size, it was the most likely guess. But when she bent to pick up one, her inside screamed. She had never seen such beautiful diamonds in her life. I mean, sure, she had collected a collection over the years, being with Rasheed, but none of the diamonds could compare to these babies. Just as she was about to act like a normal happy woman, her sense kicked in.

"So, you think this is just supposed to make everything okay? Am I just supposed to forget all you've done to me?" Rasheed was confused, but with London, he always was. It's what made him crave her more and more every day. He would usually get tired of a girl after one or two years, but with London, he felt like they had only been together for six months, although she had been his prisoner for five years now.

"No, London, I know this is not going to make everything right. But I'm trying. You embarrassed me in front of my men by allowing that little bitch to disrespect me, so I had to punish you for that. Please, what can I do to make this right?" London hesitated like she didn't already know the answer.

"I'll like to go swim with the sharks." She lied. She just needed permission to go to town, so she could go find a good doctor.

"And that's just the start." She added.

"Okay, queen, anything you want." The wet sloppy kiss sounded off as Rasheed smacked his lips onto London's cheeks.

"I'll let Tony take you." *Damn, he doesn't trust me no more. Shit! All because of that little bitch*. London's thoughts raced in her mind while Rasheed suckled on her neck.

"Okay, I want Kenya to go with me. I don't want to do it by myself." Rasheed stepped back from London to look her in the eyes.

"You don't have to look at me like that. I know what I'm saying, and I know what's at risk. And thank you for the diamonds; they're beautiful." London purposely distracted Rasheed as she slipped out of her robe, exposing her slim frame and plump buttocks. Her smooth, caramel skin looked like it was dipped in a honey pot. She was beautiful and the type of woman that dwelled in men's dreams. Rasheed couldn't help himself; he pulled London close into his space. She was just too astonishing not to touch.

"No, sir, you're not out of the dog house yet." She said, disappearing into the walk-in closet.

"Can you tell Tony I'll be ready in like forty-five minutes?" She yelled from the closet.

"Oh, and tell Kenya to get ready, and please go over your rules with her." Rasheed penis began to poke through his slacks. He sometimes loved it when London bossed him around.

"Gotcha." He yelled back.

####

Hysterical, Kenya ran full speed towards London, wrapping herself into London's arms, burying her head into her breast as she held her shaking body close. She broke down completely. She had been held in Rasheed's dark hole since she attempted to run away. London hugged her tightly and consoled her as she crumbled in her arms. Kenya hadn't seen daylight in days. Big Tony, the white guard, watched London handle Kenya so gently. He had never seen London's soft side with anyone, and to see her show so much affection for Kenya was heartwarming.

"I thought you would never talk to me again. I'm so sorry. I'm so sorry, London. You told me not to do it, and I did it anyway." Rasheed watched on from afar, and he was surprised to hear Kenya say that London told her not to run away. His queen obeying him wasn't usual, so the thought warmed his heart.

"You took me in, and I betrayed you," Kenya said.

"It's okay, Kenya. I forgive you." London responded with a knot in her throat.

"Just don't..." London couldn't bring herself to finish her sentence. How dare she tell a young girl whose life has been taken away from her to not try and get it back. She remembered her many failed attempts.

"I know. I know. I won't ever try it again!" Kenya's words cut London. Obedience wasn't something she wanted Kenya to feel like she wanted from her.

"Just hush and get in the car, girl." London knew there were too many eyes watching her, so she avoided correcting her. Kenya jumped into the jeep, and London followed her. The two enjoyed the ride to the village like they were on vacation. Everything from the fresh air to the birds chirping was soothing.

As soon as Tony and Samad began to dive deep into their own conversation, London eased close to Kenya to whisper in her ear, "I want you to pretend to have to use the restroom when we get to the village." Kenya nodded her head. She didn't ask any questions; she just agreed. She was forever in London's debt. After thirty minutes, they arrived at the village, and just as promised, Kenya requested to go to the restroom.

"Tony, the ride got to me. I have to go to the bathroom and bad." Tony took a long and demeaning look at Kenya, then said, "Go ahead." As soon as Kenya disappeared into the portable stalls, London said, "I'm going to need y'all to go watch her. We don't need any problems." Tony and Samad looked at one another; silently, they agreed. And then, together, they walked off, heading towards Kenya. As soon as they were gone, London jumped out of the truck and headed over to the hut.

31

"Hey, my name is London. Is Kentu here? The tribe of women looked at London with their mouths drooped open. They knew exactly who she was. To them, she was a wealthy snob, and even though they didn't like her, to be in her presence was rewarding, and they knew better than to disrespect her.

"Kentu, London is here to see you." Surprised, London had no idea the people of the village knew her by name. Slowly, Kentu crept around the hanging curtain with his hunting rifle.

"I come in peace, really. I don't know what you think of me or who you think I am, but I'm just a girl from the United States who was taken without permission." The expression on their faces said it all; they had no idea London was Rasheed's woman by force.

"How can I help you, Ms. London?" The hut was silent, and all eyes fixated on London. Slowly, she walked towards Kentu with her hands up, so he would know she was coming in peace. Then gently, she took his free hand and placed one of the most beautiful diamond rings in his hand.

"This is yours and much more if you can get me out of here. I need to get home. I know you know people, and I know you can make way for me to get on the boat or plane to America." London shivered, her eyes bulk wide. Kentu knew she was serious from her very spooked tone.

"I can see what I can do." He responded.

"I don't need you to see; I need you to do it. Can you do it?" London snapped.

"Yes, I can do it. Meet me here on Wednesday at this same time. There will be a cargo going out of here; I can get you on the helicopter. I'm sure the American soldiers at the clear port can help you get back home. London's heart danced with joy, and her smile brightened up the hut. The women also smiled. They were happy to see her happy.

"One more thing, where is Doctor Conner? I'm supposed to meet him here for a package."

"Doctor Conner has been gone for about three days now," Kentu said.

"Shit!" she mumbled.

"London!" Samad, Kenya, and Tony barged into the hut like soldiers, and quickly, London picked up the clothless baby off the floor.

"He's just so cute; I can't put him down." She turned and said to Tony. The women all joined in on the lie, nodding with large smiles.

"Yes, he's so adorable," Kenya added to the show. She knew without a doubt London was up to something, and she was in. She'd hoped her plan was better than hers.

"Come on, London, I think we should be going." London placed the baby on the floor and followed Tony, Kenya, and Samad out of the hut, but before she disappeared behind the curtain, she turned back to blink her eyes at Kentu. He'll never know what his head nod meant to her.

####

Finally, the moment Kenya had been dreading was here. She took one more breath, inhaling the scent of the salty ocean before the cage descended into the ocean.

"You're doing great, Kenya." Kenya thumbed London up with her shivering hand.

"Do you have my camera?" London asked through her mouthpiece. Kenya couldn't think straight. She put the camera in the wrong pocket and panicked when she couldn't find it.

"Oh, here it is." She yelled, waving the camera under the deep blue sea. Swimming with the sharks had been one of London's *to-do* on her bucket list, so she decided to tackle it while she was in Africa. She wanted to return home with something to brag about to her son and her sister.

"Thank you for coming with me, Kenya. This is something I always wanted." London's calmness was contagious, and all of a sudden, Kenya wasn't scared anymore.

"You're welcome. I'm glad I came. This is so cool." The two girls were deep down under the deep blue sea, waiting to see some of the world's biggest sharks.

"I told you, you would love it. Being under here is like being in a different world. The water is so clear and soothing." London looked around, admiring the beauty of the ocean, and out of the blue, a big grey shark appeared from behind a school of bright-hued fish, and the girls lost their cool. Kenya dropped the camera, and London burst into laughter. The look on her face was priceless; she was back to being scary Kenya.

"Get the camera Kenya, so you can take my picture." Slowly, Kenya bent down, keeping her eyes on the big-mouth shark.

"Okay, I got it. Come on!" London posed with the shark in her background. She hadn't felt this good in years. The freedom was as intoxicating as if she were swimming in vodka.

"I could stay down here all day," London said, watching the hungry shark swim about.

"Wow, you really love it down here," Kenya said as she watched the excitement on London's face. Their air bubbles made their way to the surface with every exhale; they were the only thing in the ocean that was in a hurry to leave. London could stay all day if her tank would last, but as calculated, her time under the water is mastered by the oxygen on her back. After ten more pictures and twenty more minutes, Tony had the men bring the girls back up. They went for drinks after and enjoyed the rest of their day like two free girls in a big world.

Seven

aris finally climbed out of the tub. She was good and relaxed from her hot bath. She put on a pair of black running pants, a red Spellman sweatshirt and grabbed a bottle of cold Fiji water from the fridge. She plopped down on the sofa and grabbed her laptop off the coffee table. She started back, looking at some of the shopping sites she'd bookmarked. She pressed enter, and the screen turned cobalt blue, then went completely black. She leaned over the sofa, thinking the battery must be dead, but she knew she always plugged her laptop in when she was at home, and when she looked behind the sofa, sure enough, it was plugged up.

She powered off the laptop and waited for it to reboot. She didn't hear the low blender sound. She didn't hear anything. She hit the power button again, this time praying she was not a victim of one of those apocalyptic viruses. She's got tons of irreplaceable pictures saved to her computer that she hadn't gotten around to printing yet. Nothing Paris did could resuscitate it. At that moment, she was glad she'd saved the same pictures to Kash's computer. She walked down the hall to Kash's office.

The tiles were cold on her bare feet. It pissed her off how messy he kept his office. There was a picture on the wall of Paris and Kash, and they both looked so happy as they petted their neighbor's dog, Hooch, in a photoshoot Paris made Kash participate in. Those were the good old days when Kash would do anything, even the things he hated, just to make Paris smile. On the opposite wall, Paris and Kash's wedding pictures hung. She remembered feeling like the most beautiful woman in the world.

Paris sat at his desk, a beautiful maple-colored door-turned tabletop. She clicked on the browser and typed in the last site she visited, and pressed enter, but her site wasn't what popped up. Her heart pounded as she saw before her eyes a screen full of color photographs and video clips of women giving men blow jobs and three and four of them piled on top of one man and some pleasing each other. She knew this was a porn site, but she didn't make a mistake when she typed. She closed it and retyped the same address. She couldn't believe it when she saw the same nasty people again! She did the same thing a few more times and got the same results.

Quickly, she picked up the office phone and called her best friend's son, Joshua was part of the geek squad. She explained to him what had just happened to Kash's computer, and he told her, "It sounds like Uncle Kash's computer has been hijacked. Porn sites are notorious for doing this. Over the next twenty minutes, Joshua talked Paris through a process that gave her access to temporary files, which made it quite clear her husband had been having cyber sex with hundreds, if not thousands, of women, and the mother-fucka had two names. He's Kash Jackson to Paris but King Caro to all the nasty bitches he had been jerking off with and having virtual sex with via the little webcam attachment she gave him the previous Christmas. Paris had watched porn with Kash before, but what she was looking at took things to a whole new level.

Paris's teeth felt cold. Her fists balled up on their own. She yanked open a file drawer and started rummaging through his credit card statements, only to discover he was a fucking Gold Card member. Not just on one site but on quite a few others. To the tune of a few grand a month. She sat there for the longest, more pissed off than hurt, more disgusted than anything, trying to figure out how long he'd been doing this shit. It's cheating, but Paris believed she would feel worse had she seen him with a woman versus knowing he watched them on a computer. She shut off the computer, trying to prevent stress overload.

"I will not trip over this. I will not mention this to Kash. If this is how he's been getting off, let him do it. At least it's safer than actual sex." Just as she walked to the door, the phone rang. She quickly rushed back over to the desk.

"Hello?" Routinely, Paris spoke in her sexy voice.

"Hey, baby, it's me."

"Ooh, hey, baby, what time are you getting home tonight?"

"That's why I'm calling. I'm going to be a little late tonight. These boys are not getting these plays like they should. I'm making their asses stay late tonight. We can't afford to lose this next game." Paris's ears went deaf; *I'll be a little late tonight.* She just held the phone while rolling her eyes.

"You and Cam, go ahead and eat without me."

"Okay... Bye, Kash." Paris didn't bother waiting on a response; she just hung up the phone.

"Little Kash!" her voice echoed throughout the house. She could hear his feet tapping down the hall. He busted into the office and asked the most rhetorical question, "Did you call me momma?" *Like, who else am I calling?* Paris thought as she rolled her eyes.

"Yes, go grab your night bag and put on your shoes. You're going to grandma for the night." Baby Kash jetted out of the office at full speed, screaming, "Yayyy!" all the way to his room.

####

"Paris, I can't watch him today. I'm not feeling all that well." Paris ignored her mother and jumped in the car. It was as if Stephanie wasn't even talking. Paris had gone deaf to both her and baby Kash's words. She swerved out of the parking lot at full speed. Baby Kash waved her off, but she didn't bother waving back.

In less than twenty minutes, she had arrived at the destination her GPS had told her Kash was. She'd secretly put GPS on Kash's car, but up until today, she had no courage to use it. Paris circled the Ritz Carlton hotel parking lot until she spotted Kash's Range Rover. Since he usually came home around twelve o'clock, Paris anticipated he'd walk out the front door at approximately eleven forty-five. That gave her enough time to swing around to the Starbucks entrance, turn on her hazard lights, and wait for Kash to cruise by since she "accidentally" ran out of gas.

She'd even taken care to leave her gas can at home. No need to make his job easier. If she had the real courage, she wouldn't pretend to run into him; she would just go beat down the room door and ask the questions instead of answering them. If London was here, it's exactly what she would tell Paris to do. As she waited in the hotel parking lot, she received a nod from the heavens: raindrops. A few sprinkles multiplied, falling heavier, and she began to think more than she should. *Why am I doing this to myself?*

She leaned back as *if this world was mine* by Luther Vandross played on the CD player, and tears began to run from Paris's pretty hazel eyes. She was back to feeling her lowest. After the coma, Kash had been the best man Paris could ask for. He had sworn to do right by her for the rest of their lives together, but here she was again, back crying, feeling used, unwanted, and taken for granted. "Why me, God, why?" she cried out, thinking of all the wrong in her life. She thought of life without Kash and how much better off she'd be without the responsibilities of a wife and a mother. Vacations. Her own house and space. Dates. Girlfriends outings. As the next song, *Another Sad Love Song* by Toni Braxton, came on, Paris's tears became whimpers. She was no longer tearing up in silence; she was actually boohooing. She realized that life would probably suck even more because she had no job, no passion, or no personality of her own. Before Kash, Paris was an associate at Belk.

She remembered the day she met him in Belk. The sweet memory still made her glow. She had just slit open a box of toasters in the houseware department. She gazed at the towering display rack lacking Foreman

Grills, quesadilla makers, and waffle makers. She dragged a stepladder from the corner, climbing up to make room for the just-arrived stock. As she descended the ladder, a rich baritone voice below called out, "Excuse me, are you Laura London?"

Paris sighed at the tired line she received from men and women. It was true. Her, London, and Laura London could be triplets. Same banging body. Same hazel-brown eyes. Same smile with the dimples. That same smile made men whip out their wallets and spend cash or swipe credit cards after Paris convinced them their wife, girlfriend, significant other, or boyfriend just had to have the latest gadget in their kitchen. The same smile either stopped women in their tracks while spitting out the refrain *bitch*, or made them sidle next to her and say, "My son is in the military and will be home on leave next week. Can I bring him to meet you?"

Paris steeled herself to face what she knew was an older gentleman. She formed the image in her mind: Dark. Short and stocky. Horn-rimmed glasses. Balding head. Hoodwinked. But, she turned to find a totally opposite vision: A wavy head god who stood at least six feet seven inches tall. He beckoned her to descend the ladder. He was a shade or two lighter for her taste but handsome just the same. As she climbed down, she eyed the red Nike warm-up suit that hinted at days spent at Platinum Gym.

The white muscle shirt he wore accented his six-pack abs. She got lost in those perfect white teeth, those sparkling blue-green eyes. *Our kids would have gorgeous eyes*, she thought. From that day forward, she's been trying to give him them blue-green eye babies and has yet to succeed. Never in a million years would she have thought it would be her twin to be the one to succeed. Picking herself up, Paris cranked her car up and rode off. The way she saw it, she would need a full blueprint before she could walk away from Kash. He had her heart, and he was the only stability she had. She was stuck, and there was no need to complain if she wasn't going to leave.

Eight

Spread out on the island is just about everything Paris needed to finish dinner: an array of herbs and spices, three cups of uncooked bow-tie (farfalle) pasta, two bags of frozen broccoli, two cups of shredded cooked chicken, one jar of garlic Alfredo pasta sauce and some mushrooms that had gone bad. "Dammit!" she yelled when she noticed she couldn't use the mushrooms. It was Kash's favorite part about her Alfredo pasta.

"Shit, it's no way I'm going to make it back in time from the store to finish dinner before he gets here, and I definitely can't use these. It'll kill us." The polished wooden floors squeaked beneath Paris's feet as she paced back and forth. Her last sentence, *it'll kill us* repeated four times in her head. She and Stephanie had liked to pick their mushrooms fresh from the garden, and that's what she had done, but this time, she picked some bad ones. And bad mushrooms could kill you quicker than a gunshot.

"No one would suspect anything. I have a two-hundred-thousand-dollar insurance policy out on him, and I'm sure I could live off that or flip it somehow. The house is paid for, and the cars are paid for. I should kill his ass." Paris muttered as she continued to pace around the kitchen like a madwoman. *You can do it, Paris. This is your only way out*. Her evil thoughts were loud, and she could barely hear her conscience; *what about baby Kash? He deserves a father. You're no killer, Paris; you're not a bad person. Don't be like Kash.*

"Fuck it!" she blurted as she began to dice up the mushrooms for the veggie Alfredo pasta. She stirred, chopped, and diced like a mad woman, only she wasn't mad. She had found a piece of mind. Cooking for Paris was therapeutic. She easily forgot about bad times when she cooked, especially when she knew it was for other people. The kitchen is the one place she felt the safest. She was in control of what happened there. Paris knew she was a phenomenal cook. It's her very own form of artistry. *He'll never even know the difference,* she thought.

"Shit, I'm the best cook I know. I haven't always been, but I got this shit down pack now." Paris began cooking like somebody's grandma when London turned up missing. It was a way for her to clear her mind. Accidentally, she became the best at it.

"That is it! I can open up a restaurant." Paris blurted as she thought about what she could do with the insurance money to make it multiply.

"That's what I'll do. I'll open up a restaurant." Paris placed the Alfredo in the oven and finally picked up the ringing phone. He rang at least six times she'd been in the kitchen, but since she knew it was only Stephanie telling her to come get Kash, she didn't rush to answer it.

"Why are you calling me like this? He's not my son. Call his fucking daddy and tell him to come and pick him up." She quickly yelled into the phone before Stephanie could say a word.

"Mommy, it's me. Grandma is in the hospital, and the ambulance man says you got to meet us at the Emory Hospital to get me." Paris's heart felt as if it could explode in salty tears. It was at that moment she realized she wasn't in control of her feelings. She had reacted worse than a bawling baby or a toddler throwing a tantrum. She knew she needed to get a grip on her emotions before she destroyed everything good around her.

Every negative emotion had been buried before she could even feel it, making her both passive and weak. Everyone loved her for her smile and twenty-four-seven happy character; meanwhile, every toxic feeling was crammed into her chest. The problem was that space was getting so full, so much harder to ignore, and the disparity between her outgoing personality and inner pain was so difficult to bear. She wished like hell she learned how to get her emotions out like London instead of bottling them up; she knew there would be no healthy release when the internal pressure got too high. She needed to find a way to defuse the bomb before everyone she loved got burned. How she was going to do that, she didn't know.

"Mommy, are you there?" The loud squeaky voice snapped Paris back into reality, and she nodded her head twice before she realized Kash could not see her head, "Yes, mommy is on the way." She finally uttered with a crack in her throat.

####

Stephanie's words splintered inside Paris, causing her more pain than the cancer she spoke of. "What do you mean you have cancer?" Paris managed to croak out during her whimpering.

"This can't be true!" All Paris could think about was the painful memories of David, Stephanie's long-term boyfriend. When cancer took him, he was skin and bones, pale as a ghost, face masking the trial inside. Most days, David would just scream in pain, and there was no doubting the agony. Just the thought of Stephanie enduring that type of pain scared Paris to the core. The doctors, baby Kash, the nurses, and Stephanie just watched her break to her knees. She could barely breathe. When the doctor attempted to pick her up from the floor, Stephanie waved him off. She knew Paris was harboring a lot of pain inside, and she needed just one good cry if not three rounds.

"Baby, I'm not dying. The cancer is gone. I just have to do chemo so it doesn't come back. I didn't do my chemo yesterday because I had baby Kash, so I got a little sick, that's all."

"Why didn't you tell me? I would have kept him myself. I would have gone with you. Who's been taking you to chemo anyway?" Paris snapped.

"I take myself. I catch Uber. I got everything under control. Plus, I didn't want you to worry about anything else. I don't think you can handle any more stress, Paris. Between London and Kash, you barely have time to worry about yourself." That was just like Stephanie, always looking out for the better of her children, even if that meant putting her second. You would think she birthed Paris and London out of her vagina the way she loved them.

"Momma, never keep something like this from me again." Paris finally picked herself up from the floor and walked over to Stephanie's bed.

"Promise me, you'll never keep something this important from me again. Promise me!" Paris demanded.

"I promise, baby." Stephanie's heart smiled when Paris's soft lips pecked her forehead. It had been a while since she felt her daughter's love. She and Paris used to be so close. London would be jealous. But for the past few years, it was as though Paris had taken London's spot for hating her.

"Where's Kash?" Stephanie asked.

"I don't know, momma, and don't care. I called him at least five times on my way here, and he didn't answer or bother even texting back to see what my emergency was." Paris plopped down on Stephanie's bed, and the two watched Family Feud, baby Kash's favorite show.

Nine

Hey, my London bug,

I've been writing to you, and you haven't returned any of my letters. I called you only to see you have changed your number. I'm not mad; I just only pray you're okay because Lord knows I couldn't take it no other way. You deserve all the happiness you desire. But if you're not okay, and somehow my bad doing in these streets has caught up with you, rest assured, I will not stop until I know you are safe and sound. Your happiness is always my priority. So, if you get this letter, let me know. I just want to know you're okay. I will not be mad at you for moving on, but if I don't get a response to this letter, I'm going to assume you're not okay. Just know I'm not going to rest until I find you. I'm going to set this fucking country on fire if that's what it's going to take to get you back in my arms.

London slid down into the warm water of tulip pedals. Letting it block out the sounds around her. She wished the tub would expand so she could spread her legs wilder, but instead, she just threw one over the edge of the craw foot barrel. Whenever she read the last letter Gunner wrote, she would tingle on the inside. Just the thought of him did something to her hormones. The love they shared was rare and very authentic. She knew Gunner meant every word he said; if he could, he would light up the country on fire. Only he wasn't as powerful as his ego

44

led him to believe. Rasheed, on the other hand, may have a better chance. He could probably burn the country down.

London had found the letter from Gunner in one of Rasheed's basements. Where he hid all her valuables until he found out she had found his secret spot. She assumed Rasheed took the letter from Stephanie's mailbox when he went back to the States to try and make it look like London left the country willingly to live her best life. He had made her write a letter to Paris and Stephanie saying she was okay and decided to travel the world. He then was to put the letter into Stephanie's mailbox. London remembered crying for months after that.

The water splitter and splashed as London sponged her body. She had imagined her hands were Gunner's as she palmed her stiffened nipples. She could still smell his Ralph Lauren's Blue cologne as if he was physically there. London felt her clitoris begin to throb intensely. She had missed Gunner more than anybody because he was all she had that made sense for most of her adult life. She slipped her middle finger into her juice box and swirled it around the opening of her wet but hot pussy. The deeper she dug, the louder her moans got. London was so into pleasing herself she didn't notice Kenya watching at the door. She stood stiff and silent, gawking at the beautiful sight. London didn't hear her small taps at the door, so she invited herself in. She knew she should walk back out and knock on the door, but she just couldn't pull herself away. Kenya had been secretly crushing on London since she arrived, but she knew there was no way London would find her interesting. Not because she wasn't beautiful but because London wasn't gay, and most importantly, because she was just a kid to London.

She gripped onto the warm towels she had brought for London to dry off with, trying to hold her composure. London was really into her grove. "MMMMMMMMM—MMM!!" She moaned out as she got closer to her climax. And after digging two more fingers up her hole, she exploded. Body shaking like a seizure patient. "Shit," she muttered.

Quickly, Kenya slipped back out the door to knock one more time. "Who is it?" London yelled out.

"It's me! Kenya. I brought you some warm towels and a message from Master," London burst into laughter at Kenya's joke. She had the slave accent down the pack.

"You're silly. Come in." Slowly, Kenya walked in like an intimidating young girl.

"So, what message do you have for me, little girl?" Kenya held the opened tower out in front of her, waiting for London to rise from the tub.

"He said dinner is almost ready, and he doesn't want you late." Kenya didn't blink once as her eyes were fixated on London's perfect physique. She was perfect in every way, and I could see why Rasheed was obsessed with her.

"Oh, I thought he wanted something. Go tell the old grump I'll be down in a few minutes." Kenya had gone deaf to London's words. Her mind was deep into fantasy, massaging London's breast with her tongue.

"Kenya!" London snapped. And quickly, Kenya blinked back into reality.

"Are you okay?" London asked before wrapping her body up into the warm towel Kenya held out with open arms.

"Yes, I'm okay," Kenya answered.

"Oh, okay, well, go tell Rasheed what I said. I don't want him to start thinking. Shit is never good around here when he gets to overthinking and shit."

"Oh, okay, I'll tell him." Before London could respond, Kenya had dashed out of the bathroom. *London thought that poor girl probably missed her family so much* as she dried her dripping body.

####

All eyes were fixated on London as she walked towards the long dinner table. The tail of her green velvet dress dragged behind her. Had London been in Africa by her own free will, she would have truly felt like royalty. Rasheed pampered her like a born queen. He rose from his chair as Kenya pulled out London's chair.

"Kenya, why aren't you sitting?" Slowly, Kenya slid London's chair under the table.

"Oh, she didn't tell you?" Rasheed said.

"Tell me what, Rasheed?" London's nerves rattled like a snake, she never knew what Rasheed was up to, and she'd secretly hoped that it wasn't something atrocious. She could barely stomach him torturing Kenya the way he did her on the regular.

"Kenya will be your servant from now on." Cool air released from London's mouth, blowing her Chinese bang upwards.

"I have plenty of servants already, Rasheed." Kenya stood silent by London's side, holding tea, waiting for permission to pour.

"Yes, but Kenya will be your personal servant. She will provide you with everything you need, warm towels, fresh linen, an ear to talk to, or even a massage. You can thank me later." London's head tilted back, and her left eyebrow raised, "Thank...?" Just as she was about to snap and ask, *Thank you for what*? She quickly remembered where the other girls who Rasheed had kidnapped were held captive. And Kenya was better off being by her side than being locked down in a basement where Rasheed men collected their pay. Rasheed wasn't aware that London knew about him selling girls, but she had known for a minute. She even knew about his workers impregnating them, so he could sell off their babies to wealthy families who couldn't have children.

"Thank you..." London took another one for Kenya. She couldn't understand why she felt responsible for Kenya, but she did. She could only imagine how she had to thank him later.

"Well, since she's my servant. I say she sits." London said.

"Join us for dinner, Kenya. In fact, join us every night." Kenya stood confused until Rasheed gave her permission to sit with a simple head nod. She was forever in London's debt. She didn't know why London was so kind to her, but she was very appreciative. Kenya had indulged, eating more than she'd thought possible. She started on the creamy nettle soup that felt warm in her belly; it was mossy green, with islands of orange floating through the broth. A handsome fish followed.

There wasn't any talking for the first ten minutes, only forks scraping the plates. Kenya didn't come up for air. The servants had laid a silver platter in front of her, on top of which sat a fleshy pink strip of trout garnished with dashing green herbs that Kenya didn't know but liked the taste of. In all her life, she had never had dinner like this one; her family couldn't afford it. A side plate of mussels supplemented the fish course. Their black shells laid open, the beige insides spilling out---sickening to London, who was a meticulous eater but enticing to both Rasheed and Kenya. Kenya had never eaten it before, but she's heard nothing but good feedback from close friends who could afford it.

After the seafood dishes had been cleared away, the servants returned from the kitchen with the main meal, a full spit-roasted pig, its skin a sizzling, mouth-watering golden brown, jaws prized around a forest green apple. The two servants had harmonized their heavy breathing with the screeching wheels of the cart as they'd pushed the pig to be sat in front of Rasheed. Cuts of the pork had been served with a refreshing apple sauce, easing the perfectly cooked meat down. The potatoes that accompanied it were diced up in a bowl with carrots, mushrooms, and zucchini. London only ate vegetables and fruits. The meat freaked her out, all but chicken.

After London, Kenya, and Rasheed finished dinner, he sent all the leftover food from the feast to the girls he kept hostage in a basement below his mansion.

"Oh, before I forget. I got a surprise for you." Rasheed wiped his mouth with his fancy napkin and waved his right-hand bodyguard, Obi, over.

"Bring it in," Rasheed demanded to Obi when he got closer to the table.

"Omg!" London spat out the carrots she was chewing onto her plate. *How did he find Kentu?* London thought as she watched blood leak from Kentu's mouth like a running fountain.

"I found that diamond you lost, sweetheart." London nodded her head *no* as her glistening eyes stared into Kentu's bloodshot eyes.

"What are you talking about?" She whimpered.

"This motha-fucka stole your diamond to feed his family. Big Tony tells me you played with his adorable little baby." London couldn't control her emotions, and suddenly, Kenya had lost her appetite.

"Queen, what do you think we should do to this thief?" London's big brown eyes leaked salty tears.

"Nothing, Rasheed. It's just a diamond. Just get the diamond back and leave him alone." London cried out.

"Women. They always have the biggest hearts." Rasheed said as he rose from his chair and began to walk towards Kentu.

"Do you want to tell me where you got this beautiful rare diamond from?" Kentu trembled with pain. For hours Big Tony and Rasheed had tortured him. He wasn't standing with his own strength but from the strength of Big Tony and Obi.

"Now, I don't have to remind you I don't like liars, right?" Kentu nodded his head in agreement.

"Where did you get the diamond?" London's heart pounded like African drums. All Kentu had to do was snitch on her, and he would be free. As for London, her life would probably be over.

"I didn't steal the ring, I swear. I found it in my hut. I swear to you, I'm not lying." London thought, *Yes, that's a good lie.*

"You know how careless I am, Rasheed. I told you I lost the ring. It must've come off when I was playing with the baby." Rasheed thought hard and long. He knew for sure London was clumsy with valuables because they didn't have any meaning to her.

"Please, I'm telling you the truth. I couldn't live with myself if someone was hurt because of my clumsiness." Kenya's heart pounded, and her hands shivered; she felt helpless and very scared for both London and Kentu.

"The next time you find something that belongs to me, you make it your business to bring it to me. Are we clear?" London dropped her head to the table and cried out like a baby. Only this time, she was crying happy tears.

"Thank you, Rasheed. And I'm so sorry. Please forgive me." Rasheed took one long look at London and then Kentu.

"Take him home and wrap up some of this food for his family," Rasheed said.

"Thank you. Thank you. Thank you." Kentu blurted out as he was hauled off.

Ten

"It's not you. It's me," Nasir had said to London one gloomy October day. London had fought back the tears, not wanting Nasir's up-tight family members who passed them by to see her crying. He was her first, and she'd hoped they would be together forever. He came from the type of family she had always dreamed of, and he had his head on his shoulders. A real stand-up young guy. He was a college graduate and stockbroker, with both his mother and father present in his life. But after a couple of rolls in the sack, he was ready to move on.

"I don't believe you're doing this to me," Tears rolled from London's sleeping eyes as she dreamt about the worse but best day of her life.

"Dang, stop acting like a little girl," Nasir snapped. And from thin air, Gunner intervened. London didn't know him from a can of paint. She had seen him serve some of Nasir Bougie's friends cocaine once or twice, but that was it.

"Hey, London, what's up?" Gunner had said, planting himself in the middle of their conversation. London looked confused. Gunner continued playing it cool, ignoring Nasir's scowl as he kept his eyes fixed on London.

"So, I hear you're single now," he said, flashing his pearly white teeth.

"You know, I've been trying to get with you since that day I spotted you in the grocery store." London didn't know what to say, but Nasir didn't give her a chance.

"Yo, son, for real?" Gunner towered over Nasir both in height by four inches and weight by forty pounds, so London didn't think Nasir would try to jump.

"So, are you free now?" Gunner had said, continuing to ignore him.

"We can go grab something to eat, then go see the new Spike Lee movie."

"Man, you're trying to get jacked up," Nasir said, stepping toward Gunner. Finally, Gunner turned around, looked past him like he was looking for someone, then said, "By who?" London figured now would be a good time to say something since Gunner's height and weight didn't seem to be intimidating Nasir.

"Um, I'm okay," she said, putting a hand between the guys. Gunner turned back to her.

"Not yet. But you will be. This corny ass nigga tryin' to disc you right here in the middle of a party, in front of everyone." Gunner motioned around to Nasir's family, standing around staring.

"This ain't got nothin' to do with you," Nasir said. Gunner waved him off.

"Come on, let's go. You don't need this. Or him." Before London could protest, Gunner had taken her hand and pulled her away, leaving Nasir standing next to his mother, embarrassed and humiliated.

"Sorry about that," Gunner said once they were on the elevator descending from the penthouse.

"I can't stand to see a nigga act like a bitch. How the fuck do you treat a girl you once called yours like that?"

"Thank you," London managed to say. "Thanks a lot, umm. . ." Gunner chuckled a little when he realized London didn't even know his name.

"K-Dog... Well, to you, Gunner." London and Gunner had become an idol after that day. And for the remainder of their relationship, he was her protector. Never letting harm touch her. The memory of Gunner warmed London's heart and made her smile. She was so deep into her sleep she didn't feel Rasheed gawking at her while he talked on the phone.

"First of all, I'm going to need you to watch your tone. I'm not the damn reason you're in there; I'm the reason you're getting out." Rasheed responded calmly through the phone.

"Well, what's taking so damn long? I was supposed to have been out of here. You got what you wanted a long fucking time ago." Rasheed chuckled at his livid friend. Trying to reframe from screaming, London was asleep and sleeping good for the first time in months, and he didn't want to wake her.

"Like I told you, you'll be out soon. If it was easy, you would've never needed me in the first place." Rasheed's eyes fixated on London as she began to touch herself.

"So, when are you going to get at your peoples' man?" Rasheed stared blankly at London as she caressed her breast, ears deaf to his irritated friend for a long ten seconds.

"Say, Man?" The loud screech through the phone startled Rasheed back into reality.

"I've already talked to my people'; it's done," Rasheed answered, as his eyes continued to fixate on London. She moaned lightly as her dream had drifted from the first day she met Gunner to the first time they had sex. Her dream felt like reality; she could still hear R Kelly, *sex me*, playing on the radio. She and Gunner had chilled out all that day, talking about life in general, their past, their dreams, and their future. They were only two weeks into their relationship, but they felt like they had been dating for years. They were both ready to explore each other bodies, but neither of them wanted to make the first move. Finally, after drinking the whole bottle of Grey Goose, Gunner made his move. He began caressing London's body, then he poured the soy wax from the scented candles onto her body. It was the first time London had experienced such romance. Nasir was a hit-it-and-rollover type of guy.

London moaned aloud as the memory played out in her dream. And quietly, Rasheed watched. He softly plopped down on the bed next to her with the phone pressed to his ear.

"My word is all I have as a man, and I gave you my word. Just be patient," Rasheed stuttered as he watched London's hand slide from her breast to her vagina.

"Man, I can't understand the shit you just said." Rasheed heavy African accent and stuttering words sounded like a baby babbling to his angry friend on the phone.

"I said, my word is all I have as a man, and I gave you my word. Just be patient."

London's moans increased, "Oh, I see what you got going on. Ok, I'll let you get to your business, man; just handle that for me."

"It's handled." Rasheed tossed the phone on the nearby nightstand and continued to watch the show. London had begun to finger herself to duplicate the feeling the first time Gunner had dropped his big thick dick deep into her pussy. Rapidly, she shoved her fingers in and out, in and out as she remembered wrapping her legs around Gunner's neck, grinding her pussy up towards his dick. She groaned louder as she remembered him deliberately pounding her vagina, fucking her hard and deep. After ten minutes of fingering her juice box, London frantically whimpered as her body jerked like a Honda shift stick. She had cum all over her fingers. But little did she know, she wasn't done yet. Rasheed had gotten aroused from watching her, and now he wanted his turn.

He slowly pulled back the covers and gently opened her legs. Eyes glued shut, London had yet to notice the beast between her legs. He lowered his head to taste her sweet pussy, sucking up on her dripping cum. After three licks, London finally realized that she was being sucked on in real life and not just in her dream.

As Rasheed's tongue flickered inside her pussy walls, London lay flat on the bed like a dead person. She was no longer hot and never interested in Rasheed touching her. She whimpered out when he began to finger her ass hole roughly because it hurt, but he took it as she enjoyed the pain. Ten minutes of that, and he was ready to feel her insides.

"Tell me you love me, London." Tears slowly crept from the corner of her eyes as she recited the words, "I love you."

"I love you too, baby," Rasheed did the one thing London hated with a passion, with so much passion. He kissed her. She hadn't always hated kissing; that hate didn't start until she met Rasheed. He was an African whose teeth were the color of the sun.

He put her ankles over her head, shoving his little but fat penis deep inside her pussy. As he fucked her faster and faster, she silently prayed to God, *Please, God. If you're there. Please get me home. I want to go home, God. I can't take it anymore. I miss my family. And I hate having this man on top of me.*

A bead of sweat dripped from Rasheed's sweaty forehead and onto London's quivering lip; she could have vomited at any moment. The bed began to rattle as he stroked faster and faster. He thrust his dick inside her pussy from side to side. London just ignored the pain and wiped the sweat from her lips.

"Fuck! You're like a dream come true." Rasheed said as he put one of London's leg down and straddled it while he held the other straight in the air.

"Turn around," he demanded while helping London turn to her side at the same time. Rasheed fucked London sideways to enjoy the view of his dick going in and out of her glistening juices. Her cum was all over his dick and balls and trickling down onto the silk bedsheets. Rasheed caught some of the cum running down her thighs with his finger and put it in his mouth. As he fucked her harder, more juices began to flow.

"Aww, it's coming!" he groaned out before jerking his dick from her pussy.

"Here, drink it." He demanded before shoving his dick into London's mouth. She gasped for air and gagged as he shoved his penis deep down her throat. He nutted, then she vomited. It was a routine Rasheed was used to. London threw his exhausted body to the side and ran into the bathroom to clean herself up.

Eleven

Gunner sucked in the air as if nothing had ever been so sweet. Those seven years in prison had felt like a life sentence, and he had breathed in the stale air as reluctantly as he did time. The fragrance of London grasses and meadow flowers had never been apparent to him before, but now they jumped out at him like a Victoria's Secret commercial. Nothing could make him go back to jail. He would die before he goes back.

"Where the fuck is this girl?" Speaking of the devil, Gunner turned his head left towards the loud engine sound, and sure enough, it was Cardi pushing a black matte Dodge Challenger. Cardi reached over and opened the passenger-side door as Gunner made his way to the curb.

"Hey baby," she blurted, flexing her beautiful, flawless smile.

"Where get you this mother-fucker?" Gunner plunged into the leather seats and then fastened his seat belt.

"I rented it. You know, it's easy as shit to flex in Atlanta."

"Yeah, this shit ain't nothing like New York. It's slow as hell." Cardi glanced over at Gunner as she pulled the car over to the curb.

"You drive," she demanded before jumping out of the car.

"What are you doing, girl?" Gunner asked before jumping out of the car, switching seats with Cardi. He glanced into the side-view mirror as

Cardi buckled her seat belt, hoping for a break in traffic so he could pull out and join the slow-moving parade of cars headed towards the interstate. When Gunner realized it would be a few seconds before he could maneuver the car into the street, he turned towards Cardi, leaned over, and gave Cardi a kiss on her painted full lips. They were a little damp from the Coke she was drinking, but they felt like silk. Gunner hadn't touched a woman in seven years, and he was tired of waiting.

There is a break in traffic. Cardi slides her panties down her legs from beneath her skirt and onto the floor.

"Girl, you going to make a nigga wreck." Gunner proceeded slowly in the direction of a ramp to the interstate. Jay-Z's '*Forever Young*' streamed through the stereo system. The only other noise in the car came from the wipers clearing the small droplets of rain off the windshield.

"How it feels to be free, Daddy?" Cardi asked, resting one leg up on the dashboard, exposing the visual of her vagina. She gazed at Gunner; he was still as sexy as hell. She remembered wanting him so bad back in the day, but London was all over him. She would beat bitch fast just for talking to him, but now he was free and vulnerable, and Cardi was ready to take advantage of his weakness.

Once Gunner got on the highway, the traffic was moving slowly. He relaxed a little and started talking about his plan now that he was free and all the shit he had been through in jail. He was talking, but Cardi's eyes were concentrating on his pants. She licked her lips, admiring the fact that he always filled out his pants so well, even when he wasn't hard.

Cardi began to rub her hands up and down the inside of Gunner's right thigh. He looked at her, and she gave him the look he knew all too well in return. The look that told him how much her body yearned for his touch. The highway was crowded, but they were in their own little world. The traffic had come almost to a standstill. There was an accident ahead. Cardi realized it would be forever before they made it to the room, and she couldn't wait that long. She was *feenin'* for Gunner big time.

She took off her seat belt, leaned over, and started suckling on Gunner's earlobe. The scent of Gunner's jailhouse dial soap aroused her even more.

"Girl, we'll be at the room in a minute. Chill." Cardi continued to suck on his ear and flicked her tongue in and out of the canal as she caressed his dick through his sweatpants. She wasn't stunned by Gunner's words at all; she knew he wanted it just as bad as she did. He brought the car to a complete halt long enough to bury his tongue in her waiting mouth. The car behind them blew at the horn. The traffic had started moving again. Cardi pulled away from Gunner so he could move on, but her pussy was on fire. She sat in the passenger seat with her left knee on the leather and her other leg over by the door, so he could see her *V-jay jay* while she fingered her pussy.

"Girl, you wild," Gunner mumbled as Cardi sucked her own juice off her fingers. He watched intently, darting his eyes back and forth between the road and her pulsating clit. Cardi continued to finger herself and then gave Gunner a chance to taste her sweetness off her finger.

"We're going to make a damn good team." Cardi giggled a little, then placed her head between Gunner's stomach and the steering wheel and took the head of his dick in her mouth, contracting her cheek muscles on it and drawing some of the precum out of it. Cardi wasted no time deep-throating his entire dick. Cardi knew how Gunner rolled, and she needed saving. Gunner was her meal ticket.

Gunner began shivering as he lost control of the steering wheel a little. Cardi sucked harder as she thought about how broke Big Red left her. Before she knew it, Gunner's babies were spilling into her mouth.

"Aww, shit, girl." He groaned, slipping his penis from her mouth.

"Damn, girl, you sure know how to treat a man, don't you?" Cutely, Cardi wiped her mouth and sat back in her seat. The traffic had picked up. The accident had been cleared.

"You haven't seen nothing yet," Cardi said to Gunner as he fixated his full attention on the traffic. They stopped by a Chinese spot to get some takeout on the way to their room. Once they finished their dinner, they took a long hot shower together. Gunner had been dreaming of this day with Cardi for at least six months now. He was surprised when she reached out to him on Facebook and wanted to talk.

He figured she was desperate and single because what girl wants a nigga in jail facing life, but he didn't lead her on to his true thoughts. She said she wanted her chance with him, and he went along with the shenanigans. He needed an outside connection to make some outside moves for him. The prison was the biggest hustling scene. Men in prison made more money than free niggas.

The night was more beautiful than Gunner could have dreamed it. Cardi had them set up in a suite, the rental car was flashy, and she drowned him with love. Granted, it was his money; she could have been irresponsible with money.

"Yo, how much money left?" He blurted out while watching the Hawks beat down the Cavilers.

"It's like three, almost four G's left." Gunner nodded slowly, never breaking contact with the TV.

"Aight, that'll be enough. I got to make that shit bounce."

"Yeah, baby. I know you will. You're a hustler, and that's what hustlers do. I mean, shit. Who else can beat a life sentence and get out with money like they never did a day in jail." Like an incredible hulk, monster green-like veins popped up in Gunner's neck.

"Yo, shut the fuck up! Watch what the fuck you be saying. You're bugging like a motha-fucka right now." Shocked at Gunner's words, Cardi sat, speechless. She didn't know what she said to upset him.

"What did I say?" She asked.

"All I said was, you bounced back from a real fucked up situation. I mean, shit nigga, you must have connections that none of these niggas out here have. You just walked a free man..." Cardi wasn't making matters better; she could still see the frustration in Gunner's scowl.

"Yo, don't fucking worry about all that. Period. Just change the fucking subject. Stay in your lane and be a woman." Suddenly, Gunner was calm again. He turned his attention back to the game, not muttering another word to Cardi for the night.

Twelve

"Okay. So, I'm Catwoman," Nicole whispered to Paris.

"You cannot be serious," Paris said loudly before taking another sip from the second bottle of water she had had in less than the hour they'd been outside. She was dehydrated. Atlanta's heat would certainly do that to you. They were at a yoga class but not exactly participating as they were standing outside the room, looking through the window at all the flowing bodies. They're trying to see how hard it is before they purchase a session.

"There is no way in hell I could get my body to do any of those movements."

"They're called poses, Nicole."

"Whatever. And why aren't there any black people there? You always got me doing some bougie shit, Paris."

"Maybe none of the black girls purchased a session," Both Paris and Nicole busted into laughter at Paris's joke.

"Now, shut up and watch." Ten seconds passed, and Nicole broke the silence again.

"I'm glad you came out to hang, Paris. It feels like we haven't hung in years." Suddenly, Paris's eyes glistened with water.

"I know, girl. I just have so much going on in my life." Nicole nodded her head as she watched her best friend of ten years tear up. She knew what she had to do, change the subject.

"So, I've been doing this online dating thing for a minute now, and it's really not that bad."

"You're not embarrassed to talk about it?" Paris asked with confusion painted on her face.

"No! Why would I be embarrassed? I told you, didn't I?"

"You always tell me your personal business, though. That's normal."

"I do not tell you all my personal business. Okay? Anyway, I wanted to wait until I met somebody nice, that's all. Plus, I didn't want you dogging me and making me feel desperate."

"But you are desperate, aren't you?" Paris joked. But secretly, she was the one who felt desperate for attention. She was a married woman and still craved a man's touch. Kash was lacking big time at pleasing her both physically and emotionally.

"Yeah, but so is everybody else. I mean all but you. You know, there just not enough Kash's out there in the world." Nicole joked. *Oh, trust me, you don't want one of those*, Paris thought.

"So, how long have you been doing this online dating thing, exactly?"

"About a month or two." Nicole stuttered.

"Do you really think you're going to meet somebody on an online dating service who's worth getting serious about?" *Well, shit. Kash did, so she might*, Paris thought.

"I've tried everything else."

"Like what, Nicole?" Paris crossed her arms, waiting for Nicole to come up with a decent lie.

"Okay, so I'm rusty. But you've been off the market for years, Paris. People don't just date no more. And who has parties anymore? Nobody. And I'm sure in the hell not to pick somebody up from one of these bomb-ass clubs. So, tell me, where do you go to meet a guy in our age bracket? That's on our level. Not on the street. Not at work, or you might lose your job. And not at the gym because the fine ones are gay. Shit, I'm not even sure how much I can trust the ones in church. Even the pastor out here dogging women, raping boys, and all kinds of shit."

"Okay, you made your point. Do you know anybody that's had any luck doing this?"

"Not personally, but I've read a lot of testimonials."

"You can certainly rely on those." Paris clowned.

"You know what, Paris? I'm looking at this whole thing like I do when I'm shopping and trying to find the perfect heels or the right dress. You must try on different ones and walk around in them until you find one that fits."

"If you say so, Nicole." Okay, this yoga class looks too hard. Let's check out the other one." Nicole followed Paris, and Paris followed the arrows inside the building to the flee of different classes. Once in the building, they headed down a flight of stairs. They stopped on the first landing to use the restroom, and while washing their hands, Nicole said, "This is way out of order, but I'm your friend, so I want to know. Are you and Kash okay?"

"Paris paused for a second, thinking hard about her answer. She knew if she lied, Nicole would know and just play like she believed her and then talk about it later with someone else, but if she told the truth, she would sympathize with her and maybe even keep her mouth shut about it.

"We've been better." She mumbled.

"What's wrong?"

"Well, for starters, I think we're starting to get on each other's nerves. I'm forever crying about my sister, and I just can't stop looking for her, you know?"

"And you don't have to, Paris. That's your damn twin. He's got to understand that.

"I mean, he does. But I can still tell I work his nerves sometimes about it. Plus, I'm never attentive to him when he wants to talk about work. It just bores the shit out of me now. I just don't know; honestly, my life is turned upside down right now. Some days it's good, and others, it's worse." They exited the bathroom and went down another flight, and finally reached another class. The folks behind the glass were sweating something serious.

"I know that downward dog position when I see it. They do that one a lot," Nicole said.

"Anyway, so have you tried just having a day with just you and Kash. You know, like a date night?"

"No, not in a minute." Paris sighed, blowing cool air from her mouth.

"Well, you should try that. You don't want no other woman to come slip in during y'all trying times. Honey that is the worse. You got to try and keep his attention even when you're bored and occupied." *Shit, a woman has already done that. It's too late.* Paris wanted to fill Nicole in badly on her crumbling marriage, but she just couldn't take the judgments now. Enough things were going wrong in her life. She needed to be envied somewhere.

"Oh-oh! It looks like all these sweaty and probably stinky people are headed this way. Let's get out of here." Nicole yelled before they dashed out the exit door. Looking at them, you'd swear they were about to work out. Nicole was wearing some pink-and-white getup that Paris wouldn't have chosen for her worse enemy. She had no boobs, but her ass was big enough for both of them. But Paris wouldn't dare tell her about her bad fashion choices.

"So, are we supposed to go to the salon dressed like this?" Paris asked before parting ways with Nicole.

"Yes, bitch! We just came back from working out. It's acceptable." They both laugh at the sound of them working out.

"We wanted to work out before getting our hair done so we don't sweat it out later." Paris chuckles some more.

"Girl, you come up with a mean ass story quick. That's why you, my bitch!"

"That's our story, and we're sticking to it." They both laugh aloud as they head for their cars.

####

Paris was sitting in Anthony's chair as he finished up the last touches on her lace frontal sew-in, watching Towanda, Black Keisha, and Terry weave, braid, and cut hair when Kash walked into the salon with a bouquet of tulips. She was surprised since she hadn't seen him in almost twenty-four hours. She wondered what was up because he rarely came into the salon. She prayed it was nothing bad. Then she thought about it. He was in the dog house; of course, he was at the salon. He was trying to dig himself out of the hole he had dug. He even brought baby Kash with him.

He looked so good. His body fit his white t-shirt to perfection. His smile was bright, his haircut was on point, and he smelled like a million dollars. *Damn, why can't I stay mad at this man?* Paris thought as she blushed at her two favorite men. The girls in the salon, including Nicole, gawked at Kash as he made his way toward Paris.

"Now, what are these for?" Paris said as she took the flowers from baby Kash's hand.

We just wanted to show we love you, that's all." The entire salon *Aww* in unison. Baby Kash was just too adorable.

"Well, that was sweet." Paris could barely hold it together. Kash had made every girl in the salon wish they were Paris.

"How long, Anthony man? I'm ready to kidnap this lady." Anthony ran his fingers through Paris's deep and wavy hair once more. Spinning her around in the chair just to check behind himself.

"She's all yours, man." Paris reached in her pocket for cash, but before she could find her wallet, Kash had already taken care of the bill and left Anthony a generous tip.

"Appreciate that, man."

"No problem," Kash yelled on his way out of the salon. Paris followed closely behind. As soon as they disappeared, the ladies began to talk. It was part of the normal, some good and some bad, so Nicole didn't bother getting upset.

It took every inch of willpower in Paris's body to keep from bum-rushing Kash at the door. Her heart dropped when she heard his black Jag pull up in the driveway. He had gone to wash the car while Paris got dressed for their dinner night. It was like Kash had read Nicole's mind. Paris wasn't sure where they were going, but she was just ready to spend some alone time with her husband. Baby Kash was staying with the babysitter, and Paris planned to enjoy her night baby free.

Paris walked to the door slowly; she tried her hardest not to seem pressed. Her heart melted when Kash handed her a dozen long-stemmed red roses, a box of candy, and a teddy bear holding a little red pillow that had '*I Love You*' embroidered on it.

"What is this for?" Paris asked with a large cheesy smile. She was extremely impressed with Kash since it wasn't a special day. She asked her neighbor's daughter, Makenzie, who was watching baby Kash to put the roses in a vase for her and to take them, along with the other items, up to my room. The look on Kash's face told Paris how pleased he was at the *new* Paris. Instead of being sophisticated but cute, as he always described her style, she was bad and bougie in a red spandex above-the-knee dress and black Louboutin high-heeled pumps.

They drove downtown Atlanta, and Kash surprised Paris with a horse-and-buggy carriage ride through Piedmont Park. It was so romantic, Paris didn't want to spoil the night by asking Kash where he had been, but she just had to do it.

"So, where have you been, Kash?" Ready to answer Paris's questions, Kash didn't hesitate to answer.

"I was arrested for DUI, and I didn't want to bother you, Paris. So, Josh got me out. You have so much going on these days; I hate bothering you with my bullshit."

"But I'm your wife, and you had me worried, Kash." Paris's eyes glistened, but she fought back her tears. She refused to show her weakness today.

"I'm sorry, baby. I know you were, and I'll never do that again. I can only imagine how stressed you must've been, but I wasn't thinking about that until after the fact." For about ten seconds, the two were silent, and then Kash said out of the blue, "What's this I hear about you told Kash he wasn't your child or you, not his momma or something like that?" Paris's heart dropped to her stomach; it was true. She had let her emotions get the best of her and blurted out some truth baby Kash had no idea about.

"I was upset, you weren't answering your phone, and I let my emotions get the best of me. Stephanie just told me she has cancer." Paris had to dig herself out of the hole quick, so she used Stephanie's news as a distraction.

"What?"

"My response exactly. What? She didn't want to tell anybody because... Well, you know how she is."

"Yelp. Don't want to be a burden." Kash said.

"Exactly. So, that just took me by storm, and you weren't answering your phone. I needed a babysitter. Just the whole nine." Paris teared up, and her voice began to crack.

"Don't cry, baby. I'm so sorry." Kash meant his words; the guilt was all over his face. She wanted him to feel her pain, guilt, and everything else that would make him regret his bad choices.

"What can I feed my baby to make her happy again?" he joked, speaking with his famous baby accent.

"It doesn't matter to me where you want to go. You're hosting tonight."

"Well, I don't have my mind set on nothing but that pasta at home." Paris's eyes widened like she just had seen the devil up close in person.

"Did you eat the alfredo?" Paris blurted.

"Naw, not yet, but I'm going to fuck it up when I get home."

"No, you're not. That stuff has gone bad, plus I messed it up. I'll make some more tomorrow."

"Oh, okay. Well, let's just find us something to eat out here in these streets, then." The night was beautiful, and the morning was even more beautiful. Paris woke up to some of the best oral sex ever. She didn't even have to give up no sex. After she cum all in Kash's mouth, they were off to breakfast, this time with baby Kash.

Thirteen

The room buzzed with excited chatter, and children ran between the tables in a good-natured game of tag. Then the bride and groom entered, and applause spread across the room. Everyone was happy for the bride and groom, except the bride. There was the scraping of chairs as folks got up for a standing ovation, and the forced couple made their way to the head table.

London dazzled like a born queen. She wasn't an American classical beauty, but she exceeded African standards. Her large liquid brown eyes had such intelligence and serenity that it was impossible for anyone not to be held prisoner by them. Her cheekbones weren't especially high, and her nose was round, not white-girl pointy, but there was undeniable symmetry to her features, and perhaps that's why Rasheed was so obsessed with her. But he wasn't alone. London had admirers all over Africa, and they all secretly admired Rasheed for having an American beauty tied to his empire. People say that beauty is in the eye of the beholder, but for London, that was true of everyone she met. People gaze for a split second longer than other people as their brains register surprise. Strangers gawked at her when they thought she wasn't aware. But it wasn't something that just started in Africa. Even back home, when London was a girl, her teachers favored her over the other students. In high school, she was popular without even trying.

But all the love and admiration had borne an arrogance into her. London's superiority complex gave her an ugly attitude that she made no attempt to conceal. She secretly hoped people, including Rasheed, would get the picture and eventually leave her alone for good. Just maybe the admiration would stop, but it didn't. Her assured attitude only made the people around her worship the ground she walked on.

She became more heartless and cruel-spirited with men with each passing year. The women of Africa believed she was blessed with beauty and thought she lived the ideal life. But what they didn't know was that she secretly prayed for a miracle or a fatal accident. Maybe that way, she could rejoin humanity one day.

Rasheed and London sat in front of a beautiful bouquet of baby pink roses, and then Rasheed leaned in for a kiss. There was no plastic smile pasted onto London's face. She purposely and very rudely crinkled her face with the ugliest frown. She wanted every picture the professional photographer took to capture her emotions.

The who's who of Africa was in attendance, and they were ready to celebrate. Their wedding had been a very emotional one for Rasheed and the most lavish one he's had so far. He rented out the King's castle and decorated London with four of the most beautiful wedding dresses any woman in Africa had seen. Spending a little over a million, London had the wedding of her dreams with the ugliest man on earth, both physically and internally.

There were cheers and a group of Rasheed's best men whooped aloud. After a few moments, the toastmaster rose from his chair, and everyone else sat down. The sound of his teaspoon thwacking on the side of his wineglass signaled everyone to silence except the children, who were shushed by their parents. Ten of them were Rasheed's kids, eight girls, and two boys.

"I like to say a couple of things to the bride and groom." All eyes fixated on Obi as he spoke, including Omari and Jordan. They were speechless for at least ten minutes. London was stunning and very dazzling, but she still was Paris's twin, no doubt. Just a very sparkling version.

"Say it's not so?" Jordan whispered into Omari's ears while everyone else listened attentively to Obi.

"It is so, but you must say nothing, Jordan." Confused, Jordan sat back in the chair, eyeing Omari with a vicious look on her face.

"I'm serious, this man is very dangerous, and I have to get you and Journey to safety before I approach her. I don't know where her head is. She could very much like her lifestyle here and blow the whistle on me. I got to handle this carefully." Omari leaned over to Jordan to whisper in her right ear.

"London, you are the best thing to ever happen to my brother, and I know you will wear the Okafor name with much grace and style." London could have vomited in her mouth at the sound of her name. It was true; she was now an Okafor. That name carried weight and meant everything to a lot of people around the world, not just in Africa. She was now a very unhappy wealthy woman.

"I don't think she is that happy with her new life; look at her." Jordan whispered back into Omari's ear.

"That's beside the point, Jordan. You don't know that for sure. Plus, I'm here on a mission. I need to check things out first." Omari snapped, and for the first time ever, Jordan sensed he was frustrated with her.

"Cheers to the best leader Africa would ever see." London constantly rolled her eyes, but the men of Africa didn't take offense to it. They believed all women were ungrateful, emotional, unstable creatures.

"Okay, I was just saying she doesn't look happy. I'm a woman; I know these things." Jordan whispered back to Omari before taking another look at London. She was everything and more; you could barely tell she was an American. She blended in well with the riches of Africa.

"Thank you, my man." Rasheed raised from his glass to say, speaking with his heavy African accent. Looking the best London has ever seen him look. Draped in a black classic fit Armani tuxedo. Money had a way of hiding flaws, but London could still see Rasheed ugliness even on his finest days. It wasn't his pot belly, or shine ball head, or even his popcorn yellow butter teeth but rather his ugly, inhuman actions. Any person who could sell women like they were candy on a shelf and rape and breed them like they were dogs could never be beautiful.

The entire reception, London sat quietly while people congratulated her on her new journey in life. She barely paid attention to the faces; she simply nodded her head and presented them with a semi-smile. But a voice caught her attention, "Congratulations, Ms. Okafor." Slowly, London turned backward towards the voice behind her. Sure enough, it was Rasheed's last wife, Afia.

She had a kind of understated beauty; perhaps it was because she was so disarmingly unaware of her prettiness. Her black skin was completely flawless. She didn't need expensive masks or expensive products like women in America. She was simplicity at its best. London had met her and the other two wives a couple times at the family functions, and she was always a sweet spirit. London truly believed that was why her skin glowed so stunningly; her inner beauty lit her eyes and softened her features. When she smiled and laughed, you couldn't help but smile along, too, even if it was just on the inside.

London admired her for her good spirit, even though she could never understand how she kept her sanity being with a man like Rasheed.

Instead of saying thank you, London greeted Afia, "Hey, Afia. How are you these days? I haven't seen you around the house since the baby."

"That's because you had me banned." London was beyond shocked at Afia's tone, and her confused facial expression said it.

"I never had you banned from the house, Afia." Afia gazed at the room for Rasheed before she responded to London. Sure, enough, he was across the room, speaking to guests he hadn't seen in a while.

"Sure, you did, don't act confused now. I was everything to him until you came along. Now he barely even notices me." London crumpled her face and tooted her nose, "So, you enjoy being his wife, or should I say, slave?"

"Yes, you, ungrateful bitch!" Afia kept her voice at a low pitch; the last thing she wanted to do was alarm London's heavy team of bodyguards. She was only as close to London as she was because she was one of Rasheed's wives, but even she and the other wives had boundaries when it came to London. She was the Head Bitch In Charge at all times.

"Well, I'm sorry you feel that way, my dear, but you can have this life. I don't want it, and I never got you banned." London whispered back, trying her best not to alarm Rasheed. She hated it when he was mean to the other women; she couldn't stomach it.

"You're not even the youngest, but you're the last wife. I'm the youngest, and Akua is the youngest."

"Both of yaw, no, all three of yaw are young, and you should be happy I'm taking the monster off your hands. That way, you get to live life in luxury without worrying about the monster trying to touch you." Afia's eyes gazed at the room again, then she bent down to London's chair, so she could look her in the eyes.

"He's not a monster; he's a good man. And before you, he was touching me every damn night. Now, he doesn't even look at me anymore."

"Okay, so what do you want me to do, young lady? Just tell me, and I'll do it. I swear, it'll be my gift to you. I'll give you the man wrapped in a bow if I can." London sarcastically joked, speaking like a field slave.

"You ungrateful American bitch!" Before London could finally check Afia for her rude choice of words, she quickly snatched the knife off the table and held it to London's throat.

"I want to slice you thin, little miss perfect." London didn't blink, scream, or flinch. She badly wanted Afia to get it over with. But Rasheed and the guards, on the other hand, were ready to blow Afia's head right off her body. The chatter in the room increased as all eyes were fixated on Afia and London. Roughly, Afia snatched London up from her chair.

"I don't hear talking now!" Afia said.

"Go ahead. Do it!" London blurted out. London's personal team of bodyguards quickly approached London for rescue, but Rasheed waved them off.

"Afia, if you don't put that knife down, you're going to have hell to pay. Think about your daughter, Hope." Slowly, Rasheed walked up to Afia. Before reaching her, he took the .45 from Big Tony's hip.

"She's our child. Do you see what I mean? You don't pay us any mind since this bitch came into your life, and she doesn't even appreciate you."

"If you don't let go of my wife, you ungrateful little bitch, I'm going to cut your daughter's throat in front of you." Afia knew Rasheed wasn't lying. He didn't lie. Life as she knew it was over, but she wanted to make sure he knew how she felt, and she knew if she could touch London, she could touch Rasheed. Quickly, she threw London to the floor and snatched the gun from Rasheed the moment he charged her.

"So, what are you going to do with that?" Rasheed asked her as she aimed the pistol at his face.

"I should wipe out your existence, but she would love for me to do that," Afia looked over at London, who was slowly rising from the floor. "Wouldn't you like that, miss perfect?" London answered Afia with a devilish smile. She wished like hell Afia had pulled the trigger on Rasheed's ass. But instead, she turned the gun towards herself, shoved it in her mouth, and pulled the trigger. Both London and Kenya, who was now at her side, dropped to their knees. Face covered with shock.

Quickly, Omari ran over to Afia's side to check her pulse.

"Leave her there; if she isn't dead, she will be soon." Rasheed held his hand out to Omari.

"You must be my new doctor?" Omari looked up from the floor to Rasheed. At this point, he, too, was covered in Afia's blood.

"Get up and greet me; she'll be fine. My men will take good care of her." He joked.

"I'm Omari," Jordan watched Rasheed's every move from the sideline. She wasn't sure how fond Omari Rasheed was. God forbid he did something to him to try to save Afia.

"I know who you are." Rasheed shook Omari's hand like the blood on them was just water.

"Sorry for the blood," Omari said before grabbing a napkin from the nearby table to wipe some of the blood from it.

"Oh, that's okay. I'm used to getting my hands dirty." Rasheed and his collection of men friends burst into laughter. Murder was something. They weren't the bit least stunned. London, on the other hand, was terrified. She couldn't believe what had just transpired, and like Afia planned, London was going to think about her for the rest of her life.

Kenya held London's trembling body in her arms as she screamed out, "Oh my God! I want to go home. I can't take this anymore." The wedding party watched as she lost her mind. Whimpering out some of the craziest things. Finally, after ordering his men to take care of the mess surrounding him, Rasheed made his way over to his new wife.

"I got her from here. Thank you, Kenya." Hesitantly, Kenya turned London over to Rasheed. He squeezed her tightly in his arms. He knew Afia had severely shaken her up, and for the first time in over a decade, his heart pumped for someone other than himself.

"I'm sorry, I let her do that to you." He said, rocking with her body side-to-side.

"I'm going to make this up to you, I promise." London just whimpered; she didn't respond to anything Rasheed said. Meanwhile, the entire wedding party watched the drama from afar, that's until they were instructed by the bodyguards that the party was over and that they had to go home.

"We got to help her, Omari." Jordan said to her husband on their way out of the door to their car.

"I know, Jordan. I must wait until the time is right. You and Journey are my priority. And I don't want you saying a word to Paris about this."

Jordan knew Omari was serious, plus she agreed. Rasheed was a big fish to fry.

"I promise, baby, I won't say a word."

Fourteen

The sun shone luminously, and the color of the spring day under its glare was offensively bright and cheerful. It was as if Afia conspired to show London that she was resting peacefully. It was as if the world was going on without Afia, and London felt it shouldn't. London felt everything should be as grey and foggy as her emotions; it should be cold and damp with silent air. But the birds still sang, and the flowers still bloomed.

London walked through the churchyard like a silhouette of herself, wishing she really was as insubstantial as the shadows so that her insides might not feel so mangled. As London took a seat near the front, the long-held-back tears began to flow. London was not ashamed. She always liked Afia. Now she was gone. A light had been extinguished forever in London's heart. She sat in her silent grief, rocking back and forth, and awaited the start of the funeral services that were held outside in a field surrounded by nature.

The preacher's words were well-spoken, and the speeches from the other wives and friends who were servants brought out a fresh onslaught of tears. London struggled to hold back some of her grief, but her tear flowed silently, sliding down her immobile face. She felt bruised on the inside, numbness, emptiness. *It should be Rasheed in the casket,* she thought. Not a sweet innocent girl who was manipulated into believing that a monster like Rasheed was worthy of her love.

Both Akua, Rasheed's first wife and Akinyi, his second wife, broke into loud, uncontrollably sobbing when the pink casket lowered into the grave. Everyone dressed in black threw dusky pink roses on the casket. Funeral etiquette demanded London offer the family, well in Afia's case, close friends, her condolences, but she knew the wives hated her gut. Akua, who was only thirty, and Akinyi, who was twenty-eight, didn't want to hear from her. She watched them mean mug her through her tear-strained eyes.

She couldn't understand how they didn't see she wasn't the enemy. She was only Rasheed's wife by force, just as they were before they fell in love with the beast. London desperately wanted to provide sympathy and comfort to the wives because she knew how close they were to Afia. But so was she, and no one seemed to care. London looked after Afia like she was her baby sister. She had saved Afia from beatings many times, just as she did with Kenya, but no one credited her for her good deeds.

Just be the bigger person, London, she thought as she lifted from her seat in pursuit of the wives. Grief tore at her insides like a tornado as she slowly walked towards the ladies; before she could reach them, her tears fell thickly, and her voice became stuck in her throat. Maybe this wasn't the time to mend fences. Some people just needed space before seeing the good or the truth, she thought. All things considered, she turned back around as Kenya helped her walk back down the path to the car. Perhaps a permanent distance would be the better option, she concluded, and before getting into the car, she heard her name echo across the field.

"London!" Akua yelled out, running to the car.

"Yes?" London turned to say.

"I just want you to know Hope is now your responsibility." Confused, London looked around for Rasheed.

"It is tradition." Akua took Afia's baby girl, Hope, from Akinyi's hand and handed her over to London.

"What is tradition?" Baby Hope screeched out, hollering like a baby in distress as Akua attempted to give her to London.

"I'm not getting a baby; what are you talking about, lady?"

"She's your baby now!"

"Akua!" The ladies' heads turned toward the sound of Rasheed's voice.

"Take baby Hope with you."

"But, Hope is her responsibility now and...."

"Do as I say and nothing more!" Rasheed blurted out before Akua could finish her sentence. Both London and Akua stared at each other until the car was no longer in sight. She was off to a honeymoon with a husband she had no intentions to love.

####

"Welcome to Zambia." London was in awe.

Victoria Falls was known as the greatest curtain of falling water in the world. London had never seen anything more beautiful. It was Niagara Falls times ten. Not that she had ever been to Niagara Falls before, but the pictures had nothing on this view.

"It's so much water," London said as she spun around in awe of the scenery.

"Did you know more than five hundred million cubic meters of water per minute plummet over the edge, over a width of nearly two kilometers, into a valley over one hundred meters below?" The tourist guide was happy to fill London in on Victoria Falls's greatest facts. She was his meal ticket. He knew Rasheed was filthy rich; if he made London happy, he made Rasheed happy. And that could equal a charitable tip.

"No, I didn't know that. I just know I have never seen something so beautiful. Will I be able to see this beautiful view from our room?"

"Oh, of course. Columns of spray can be seen from miles away at the height of the rainy seasons."

"Do you like, beautiful?" And just like that, London was brought back to reality. Rasheed pot-belly rubbing up against London's mid-back wasn't pleasant at all. She had wished she was enjoying this beautiful view, this once-in-a-lifetime experience with Gunner, but no, she was stuck in La La Land with the beast.

"Yes, it's beautiful." She muttered before snatching loose of Rasheed.

"Now, you'll be staying on the Zambian side of Victoria Falls. Many of the accommodation features beautiful views of the Zambezi River, hostels, backpackers, campsites, lodges, 24h reception rooms, concierge services, wireless internet, satellite television, and room services." Charles, who was clearly an African American, was talking so fast London wondered if Rasheed had heard him say the magic words. She glanced over at Rasheed, and he wasn't paying her or Charles any mind. He was talking to the bag handler, making sure he didn't lose any of their bags.

"Did you say Wi-fi?" London whispered. Charles looked over at Rasheed and then back at London, who had pulled out a hand full of money and placed it in Charles's hand.

"Yes, free wi-fi," Charles whispered back before leading London to her and Rasheed's room.

"Hold up. Hold up!" Rasheed blurted out, running behind London.

"What? What's the matter?" London turned to say.

"Nothing. Nothing is wrong. Here, put this on." Suspiciously, London looked at the blindfold, confused. *What has he got up his sleeves now?* She thought as he tied the blindfold on her head.

"Why are you blinding me, Rasheed?" Slowly, London walked with Rasheed's guidance. She waved her hands out in front of her, not trusting Rasheed's support. Once inside, Rasheed told her to open her eyes. She was shocked to see a king-size bed adorned with huge, fluffy pillows and wildflowers wrapped up in ivy flowing around the bedposts. There was also a small bouquet of wildflowers sprawled across the bed for her. It was beautiful, only she didn't want to enjoy it with Rasheed.

I guess this is how the ladies fell in love with the beast. Well, it will not happen to me. I refuse. I will not. London's thoughts took on a conversation of their own until she heard Rasheed say, "Oh, yes, before I forget. We won't be needing that Wi-fi. You can turn it off. We're on our honeymoon. We don't need any distractions." Rasheed words were worse than bullets. London would've rather been shot than have another line of hope taken from her. Just as she thought she was one foot ahead of Rasheed, he snatched that hope from her. She was stuck in a beautiful place with an ugly man who craved to touch all over her. And if that wasn't enough, she was told that she indeed had to step up and be baby Hope's mother. She wasn't given an option or explanation, just a demand.

Fifteen

aris was lying in bed watching reruns of '*Martin*' when the phone rang. "Hello," she said after noticing the number was blocked on the caller ID. She prayed it wasn't a telemarketer. If so, as soon as she heard the unfamiliar voice ask for her, she would do what she always did and hang up.

"Is this Paris Jackson?" a woman who was obviously Latina asked. She also had a west-coast accent. Kash had family spread throughout the west side. Maybe this was one of them.

"Who wants to know?" Paris asked. She sat up straighter and pressed MUTE on the TV remote.

"Hennessey Vasquez."

"I don't know anyone by that name."

"Well, you do now. You might want to sit down, honey."

"Why?" Now Paris was beginning to feel curious along with wary.

"I just want to know how long you have been seeing my man?" Paris didn't think she'd heard her right. She couldn't have.

"You must have the wrong number. I'm a married woman. Goodbye."

"Hold on a minute! Is your husband's name Kash Jackson?"

Yes, it is, and I'd really like to know who you are, how you got my number, and why you're calling my house."

"He's both of our man, sweetheart. I got your number off one of his cell phones right after he called you last night. He did call you last night, didn't he?" Paris thought about the night before; indeed, Kash had called her last night. Paris pressed the OFF button on the remote, swirled her legs off the side of the bed, and stood up. She didn't think this shit was funny.

"He was out on business last night. But what business is it of yours?"

"Well, I hate to break it to you and completely unexpected and everything, but there's no decent way to tell you this: I'm pregnant with your husband's baby. Paris inhaled but couldn't breathe out. She started fanning to generate some air, even though the ceiling fan was whirring high above her.

"You still there?"

"Is this some kind of prank?" Paris asked after finally being able to exhale.

"What would I get out of it?"

"I don't know. But I don't believe this bullshit. Maybe he fucked you, but I doubt very seriously he would get you pregnant. So, what is it you really want?"

"He's the liar and the cheat, honey, not me. I just accidentally found his other wallet under the car's front seat when I took it to the car wash, and there was your ID and your little family portrait. I didn't even know he had a family. I couldn't understand how he had a whole family when he was always with me."

"You know, I don't have time for this," Paris said as she got up from the bed and started walking around in circles. Her head was beginning to feel like it was full of cotton. She badly wanted to hang up, but her curiosity was on a high. She flopped back down on the bed, dug her toes into the snow-white carpet, and decided to listen, if for no other reason than entertainment.

"How long have you been married to him?"

"That's really none of your business. Why don't you tell me since you seem to know so much about us?"

"Not *us*, him," she snapped. I can prove this is no childish prank, sweetheart. Ask me something about him. He loved fish and grits; his favorite color is red, and he liked his dick sucked while he took a shit." Paris knew Hennessey wasn't lying, Kash had once asked her to give him head while he took a shit, but she refused, and he never asked again, but she could tell from the sounds of things that Hennessey didn't turn him down.

"He told me you couldn't have kids and that you were a twin." Paris listened to Hennessey; it was all too surreal. She knew now without a doubt that this girl, who sounded no more than twenty-three or twenty-five at the most, wasn't lying.

"Listen, I don't know why you are calling me because I can't give you no child's support. I don't care what Kash does when he's not with me, and finally, I'm his wife. I'm not going anywhere. So, if you can't get in touch with him, too bad. Join the rest of them. I don't care, as long as he brings his ass home and pays these bills." Suddenly, Hennessey was quiet; Paris could tell she had hit her spot. She had won the battle, but the war had just begun. She now had to fight with Kash when he got home. She hung up the phone before Hennessey could respond because she didn't want to give her the room to come back.

####

This happened three years ago. To Paris, it sometimes felt like yesterday. Kash had called Hennessey back in front of Paris to prove his point that she was lying about the baby but not about their affair. She confessed to lying, or he made her tell a lie about telling the truth; either way, Paris had never heard from her again, but every time she woke up to Kash gone on Saturdays, she assumed he was out with another chic.

85

"Fuck!" she said when she opened her eyes and looked around her bedroom. A wave of fear paralyzed her, and she couldn't move. Her heart was racing as if she had been running. Her forehead was wet, and so were her pajamas. It's not from night sweats. Her hands were tingling, but she couldn't shake them. Not yet. She could blink, which she does until she's batting her eyes—anything to send the past back where it came from.

She dreams about Kash cheating from time to time, but most times, her bad dreams are about London. Occasionally, the dreams show up and shake her up a bit. When they do, she waits the five or ten minutes it takes for her breathing to slow down, and she can feel the blood flowing into her fingertips.

The sun was peeking through the space between the shutters. Paris knew she needed to get up, so she could go take Stephanie to chemo. Not that she had asked her to, but she wanted to surprise her. With baby Kash at his friend's house and big Kash out doing God knows what with whom, she had free time to spend with Stephanie.

"Get up, Paris, get it together." She counts to three, rolls on her side, and opens the drawer to the night table. She reaches for the two prescription bottles. Swallows the Zoloft dry. She remembers the promise to herself that she would stop taking them, but at least she could finish the bottle since she paid good money for them. Her doctor had stopped prescribing them to her months ago out of fear that she would start abusing the privilege. He advised that she get counseling because she was clearly going through a lot. *But what about the pain in the meantime?* Paris thought before buying the prescription drugs off the street.

Next, she grabbed the Xanax. When she shakes it, nothing rattles? "Okay, that's it for that, Paris. You are not a junkie," She mumbled on her way to the restroom.

####

The doctor's office was packed. Both Stephanie and Paris sat quietly, slouched down in their chair, flipping through magazines, waiting for Stephanie's turn. The room was overflowing with a bunch of white and black women who had breast cancer. They were all bald with stress on their faces.

Paris gained a new-found love for doctors and nurses after watching them deal with cancer patients so gently. They were all so patient. They walked around with genuine smiles pasted on their face.

"Paris, I told you. You don't have to stay. Just come back and pick me up."

"Momma, I don't mind. I told you. I cleared the day out for you."

"Well, take the time and go do something nice for yourself." Paris wanted to snap at her mother like she was used to doing, maybe yell out something that meant, *that's why we never try to do anything for you. You don't know how to accept help with your ungrateful ass,* but she knew that this wasn't the time or place. Plus, Stephanie could have had her own reason for wanting to deal with this scary tragedy alone.

"Are you sure, Stephanie?"

"Yes. I'll be good. I'll call you when I'm done." Without uttering another word, Paris grabbed her purse and headed for the door.

"Oh, and Paris?" Stephanie yelled out before Paris disappeared behind the double doors.

"Yes, Stephanie?"

"Thank you. I really appreciate you bringing me here." Paris didn't know why, but she was suddenly feeling like a little girl. Tears wanted to burst out of her hazel-brown eyes and down her face, but she held them back.

"Don't be silly, chic. You don't have to thank me." Paris joked before pushing one of the double doors open. Quickly, she fetched her car before the tears began to show themselves to the public.

"Ms. Jackson? Wait up!" So, caught up in her mission to ditch the hospital, Paris didn't realize the lady chasing her to her car.

"Ms. Jackson?" The lady said, catching Paris's car door before she could shut it.

"Who are you?" Paris snapped with a wrinkled forehead and a tooted nose.

"Hey, I'm Kimberly Coffin. You don't know me, but I'm a New York reporter, and I'm currently doing a segment on missing black and Latina women. I will love to have a word with you about your missing twin sister. In fact, I was wondering if you would be interested in talking about her case on TV?" Paris had waited what seemed like forever for this moment, and finally, it was here. For the longest, she had been trying to get news coverage about London.

She had the local's attention for a good two weeks or maybe a month at the most, and that was it. No one cared to cover the story anymore. They were all looking for a happy ending to wrap up the missing story, and Paris had none. Years later, she was still looking for her missing twin sister.

"Yes, sure. I'm interested." Kimberly smiled and then reached into her purse for her business card.

"Here, give me a call, and we can link up." Paris returned the smile, flashing her glistening eyes.

"Will do."

"Good. I'll be looking for your call."

Sixteen

Egypt nervously sipped away at her third glass of wine. Her eyes peered out the window, but instead of taking in the beauty of New York City, she was watching every person who approached the front door, anxiously awaiting her blind date, Kevin.

After Marcus, Egypt swore she would never date again. She had lost good friends and family members over him. It took her years to get him out of her system, and she was proud of herself. She had wished her one true friend had seen her doing her thing on the dating scene. London had told her a million times Marcus was no good, and she didn't believe her. Every time she thought about how their friendship ended, it cut her soul deep.

After an hour or so, she finally spotted her date walking through the door. She knew it was him because he was supposed to have on a red shirt and jeans and indeed this guy had a red Polo shirt and a nice pair of jeans. Egypt stood up and waved him over. The last time she talked to him, she was giving him phone sex. The memory shot through her mind as she hugged him hello.

"I'm sorry I'm so late. It was like a forty-five-minute drive from where I'm coming from."

"Oh, I know. It's okay; I'm in no rush. I just love this restaurant. Plus, I feel comfortable meeting you in my neck of the woods." Both Kevin and Egypt laughed as they took their seats.

"I see you've started without me," Kevin said, pointing at Egypt's wine glass.

"Yes, I've had a couple." Egypt joked, twirling her wine around in the glass.

"You're living in Manhattan, right?"

"Yeah, but that's not where I'm coming from, though. I was over at a friend's house."

"Oh, okay." Egypt was so nervous; her shaking legs shook the table.

"I got to say, you're much more beautiful in person." Egypt blushed like a schoolgirl, twirling her kinky blonde curl around her index finger. And then suddenly, she saw a ghost. Her heart drops into her stomach.

"Oh, I don't even believe this shit." She mutters before she sips another sip from her glass.

"What are you saying?" Kevin said. It was as if Kevin didn't exist. He had vanished, and Egypt's eyes fixated on Gunner, and the one girl London and Egypt couldn't stand, Cardi. Gunner took off his shades and sat down at his reserved table. For the first time in years, Egypt got to look him in the eyes. The whole of Brooklyn knew he was the reason London got snatched up in the first place. It broke Egypt's heart to see Paris on TV crying for her sister. No one even knew Gunner was out, let alone flaunting around London's enemy. *How dare he disrespect her that way?* Egypt thought before jumping up from her table.

"Excuse me for a second." Kevin was confused at Egypt's sudden attitude change. His eyes followed her across the room to Gunner's table.

"You slim ass nigga!" Eyes from all over the restaurant fixated on Egypt.

"Bitch, could you be any more ghetto?" Cardi snapped.

"Bitch, don't say shit to me. You raggedy-ass hoe! You couldn't wait till my girl was gone so you could get up under her nigga."

"Girl, her nigga found me." Cardi blurted back.

"Man, yaw, chill out with that shit." After checking out the scene and finally seeing that Egypt wasn't returning to the table, Kevin walked over to the table to attempt to bring Egypt back to their table.

"You are a punk ass nigga, Gunner. London out here missing in the world, and you sitting here living the life when everybody and their mommas know, you're the fucking reason she's missing!"

"Yo, ma! Talk about what you know. You don't know what I got going on. You don't think I'm thinking about her missing." Words flew from Egypt's mouth that she never thought she'd even think, let alone say out loud. She knew instantly from the look in his eyes that her words hit their mark. In that instant, the tension in the room grew intense. Kevin tried to pull her away, and Egypt shoved his hand away.

"Yo, you better get ya, girl, bruh!" Gunner yelled out to Kevin. Egypt would have assumed that Kevin would be scared since he was uptown, but he didn't display a scary bone in his body. He actually stood in front of her like a brick wall.

"You're a buster ass nigga, Gunner. London damn near devoted her life to your ass."

"Bitch, you out of line!" Kevin quickly walked up to Gunner.

"Listen, Buddy, I don't know what the fuck is going on, but the name-calling not going to fly."

"Man, you betta bag the fucked up partna." The restaurant owner walked over just in time to calm down the brawl.

"What's up, Hernandez?" Gunner knew the owner personally. The spaghetti joint was his and London's favorite spot.

"I got to ask you to leave, Gunner." Confused, Gunner snatched away the hand he was about to dap Hernandez down with.

"What do you mean?" Gunner snapped.

"I mean, you got to go. I can't condone this. London was my girl, and I can't even believe that you would come in here with this girl on your arm."

"What mean, that girl?" Cardi blurted.

"Just like I said," Hernandez answered.

"Man, let's bounce. I don't have time for this shit." Gunner looked around at everybody who was looking at him sideways--- Kevin, Egypt, and Hernandez and he felt like a chump. He grabbed Cardi by the arm, and they swiftly walked out of the restaurant.

"I'm so sorry for putting you in such a fucked-up situation." Egypt turned to Kevin and said.

"It's cool. I would have done the same thing for my friend. I respect you for that. Maybe, you can tell me more on our next date."

"Sure, no problem." Egypt was surprised to hear that Kevin was still interested in her after her ghetto outburst.

####

"I'm so sick of this shit with you, Gunner. Everywhere we go, somebody got something to say. What is the deal with London anyway? You got niggas pulling up on me with pistol and shit, talking about making sure your man knows what his responsibility is." Cardi threw her purse to the floor as soon as she entered her and Gunner's new apartment.

"If we going to continue this shit, I need to know what the fuck is going on. I can't be in the dark no more." Without warning, Gunner pulled Cardi close and thrust his tongue down her throat. He knew there was nothing in this world that she loved more than sex. Their clothes came off quickly, both ripping at the other until they were completely naked in the dimly lit living room.

Cardi took one of her fingers and rubbed it against her clit, taking it and putting it into Gunner's mouth, letting him savor her juice off it. She rubbed her fingers against her clit again, this time sucking her own juice off her finger. Then they began to kiss again, both savoring her sweetness at the same time.

Gunner pushed Cardi on the sofa on the desk so that her head was hanging halfway over the arm of the chair, and her nipples were protruding upward into the air. He suckled on them one at a time, not only taking her dark pearls into his mouth but licking the entire breast, starting at the base of each one with the tip of his tongue and making light, circular strokes until he reached the hardened prize. She was in ecstasy. And just like that, she had forgotten about the argument with Egypt. That's until Gunner mumbled out, "Oh, London. You are so sweet."

"London?" Aggressively, Cardi threw him off her. Gunner tumbled onto the floor.

"Man, you are tripping. I didn't say no damn, London."

"Yes, you did. You just called out her name, Gunner!" Guilty as charged, Gunner put back on his clothes and quickly charged towards the door before Cardi could stop him.

"I don't have time for this shit, man!" Gunner slammed the door behind him, and Cardi broke down in tears.

Seventeen

Paris slowly drove through the neighborhood streets, searching for a parking space close to Piedmont Park. It had been about four months since the last time she'd been to this area, and already the cost of parking had doubled and, in some cases, tripled.

"Shit, look at the price of parking for that lot!" Paris shouted.

"They must think this is New York or some shit," Paris mumbled as she finally found a parking spot near Grady High School, just only a couple of blocks away from the park.

"Shit, I know this lady is wondering where I'm at. Come on, Kash. We got to hurry up." Quickly, Paris and baby Kash jumped out of the car.

"Don't forget your bag, Kash."

"I got it, mommy." Swiftly, Paris and baby Kash walked to the park, where they found Kimberly enjoying the view on a bench under a tree.

"Hey, I'm so sorry I'm late," Paris said, extending her hand out for a shake.

"Oh, you're okay."

"Have you been waiting long?" Paris asked.

"No, not that long. You're okay. I'm in no rush. Plus, this is a beautiful park."

"Traffic was so crazy," Paris added as she helped baby Kash unpack his activity bag.

"Hey, little man," Kimberly said, squeezing Kash's cheeks.

"Hey," he blushed.

"Kash, you can put on your skates, or you can play with your ball."

"Okay," Kash picked up the skates and sat on the bench next to the one next to Kimberly and Paris.

"Don't go too far now."

"Okay, I won't."

"I'm sorry, Kimberly. Okay, let's get to it. Where do we start off?"

"Well, first, I want you to fill out this questionnaire. It's questions about you and your sister's bond. Facts about her last days with you, etc. Then we'll go over this information and facts about her case on camera. I just like to give the questions on paper before doing the live show, so you'll know what you're up against."

"Thank you for caring," Paris said.

"Oh, no problem. I know this must be a very trying time for you."

"Yes, it is. Kash! Be careful, baby." Paris juggled talking to Kimberly and watching baby Kash, and as if she needed any more distraction, her phone buzzed in her hand, notifying her that a voicemail had been received.

"I'm sorry, Kimberly; I'm usually not this busy." Paris joked.

"I got to listen to this. Do you mind?" Kimberly shook her head, then waved her hand before saying, "Go ahead."

Paris dialed her voicemail, and what a surprise, it was Egypt. *"Hey Paris, this is Egypt. I would ask how you are doing, but that would be rhetorical. So, I'll just get straight to it. Gunner's out of jail, and he's in New York, living like he's never left the streets. Oh, and get this, he's flaunting around the one girl London couldn't stand. Anyways, I thought you should know. Give me a call back as soon as you can.*" Tears slipped from Paris's eyes without permission. Kimberly couldn't help but notice.

"Is everything okay, Ms. Jackson?" Quickly, Paris wiped her eyes.

"Yes, I'll be fine. It's just if it isn't one thing, it's another. It's like as soon as I make one step forward, I get pulled one step back."

"Is this about your sister?" Kimberly sat back down next to Paris on the bench. She could tell Paris needed some comforting, and she wanted to ease in before outright hugging her.

"Yes, that was her best friend from New York. She says my sister's boyfriend is out of prison, and he's flaunting around the same girl; my sister couldn't stand. It's like he's just erased her when he's the reason she's missing in the first place." Paris fought back her tears, but she could barely see clear through her wet glazy eyes.

"Did you say he's the reason she's missing?" Paris lounged back on the bench.

"Yes, we believe the guy he owed money took my sister, but we don't know much about the guy, and Gunner's hasn't been any help." Kimberly listened intensively, nodding her head. Then suddenly, it hit her.

"You know what? I have some old cop friends in New York who could stop by Gunner's place and shake him up a little about this guy he owes. Would you like me to send them by his place?" It was as if Paris had seen the light at the end of a tunnel. She lifted her head up and wiped her eyes before her tears could drip.

"Would you do that for me?" Paris asked.

"Yes, sure. Just ask her friend to give you the address, and I'll set it up." Kimberly said.

"Cool. I'll do just that." Paris jumped up from the bench and hugged Kimberly tight.

"Thank you so much."

"You're welcome. Now you stop worrying and spend some time with the little man over there. You have my number; just call me as soon as you get the address." Kimberly waved bye to baby Kash and then fetched her car. As soon as she was out of sight, Paris called Kash to fill him in on her day, but he had no time. He was in the middle of a business meeting, so he says. Paris knew that was code, for he was with one of his play toys.

She watched baby Kash play, holding back her tears until she couldn't anymore. Quietly, she bent her head to her knees and released all her frustration. Sobbing like a little baby, only she wasn't loud.

Kash could tell she was crying with one look over at his momma and baby. He knew her all too well. It wasn't the first time he had seen her break down. Although she always tried to hide it.

"Momma, don't cry. It's going to be alright." Kash's warm hug was more comforting than he could ever understand.

"Aww, baby, that's so sweet. But I'm okay. You can go play; you don't have to worry about me." Paris couldn't understand how baby Kash could be so loving and caring when all she's been is mean and distant from him in the past couple of weeks.

"Oh, that's okay, momma. I don't want to play anymore. Let's go grab something to eat." Kash flashed his snag-a-tooth smile, and Paris couldn't resist; she swarmed him with kisses.

"Momma, not in public." He joked, laughing as she tickled his stomach.

"Let's go. I think I want some Waffle House; what do you think?"

"Sounds good to me!" Baby Kash blurted, rolling behind his momma on his plastic four-wheel skates.

####

It's never good news when a police officer comes to your door at 3am. It's even worse when they don't ask to come in but instead just invite themselves in. At that moment, Cardi knew she was about to be hassled,

97

and the first person who came to mind was London. London had been a pain in her ass even while she was gone.

"Where's Gunner?" The police officer who was clearly in charge said as soon as he entered the lavish apartment.

"I'm right here; who wants to know?" Gunner appeared from the back room like a ghost, and quickly the four officers reached for their guns.

"I want to know." The officer responded, pulling his gun from the holster.

"And who the fuck is you?" Gunner snapped.

"Your worse nightmare if you don't give me the answers I'm looking for." The officers searched the house as if they would find London somewhere stashed away.

"Where is London?" The leading officer asked.

"You'll think if I knew, she'd be missing?" Gunner had dealt with the police all his life, so he didn't scare easily. Meanwhile, Cardi was scared out of her mind. She knew that this London situation was bigger than Gunner had been leading on. Butterflies swarmed around in her gut, and her palms were sweaty. She knew London was nowhere in the apartment, but the officers searching the house made her second guess the facts.

"Seems as though you've moved on." The thinnest officer, whose name badge read Michael, said as he looked Cardi up and down.

"Well, looks can be deceiving." Gunner mugged the officers showing no fear.

"So, who is this guy that you owe, and where is he?"

"You think if I knew that, he'd still be breathing?" The officers circled Gunner like he was bait, but he didn't bulge, blink or flinch.

"If you love London like you pretend to, then tell us something that could be helpful. Her family is worried about her, and her kid misses her." Gunner's eyes watered, and he felt as though his heart had dropped into his stomach.

"Her kid?"

"Yes, her son." From the confused look on Gunner's face, the officer could tell Gunner had no idea London had a kid.

"Oh, you didn't know? Yes, she has a baby boy." Gunner's nerves rattled, but he didn't show any signs of it. He hid his shaking hands in the pockets of his Ralph Lauren pajama pants.

"So, you see, anything you know could help us bring her home to her family. Tell us where this dude at, and we won't mention you when we find him." The third officer, Raymond, added.

"Like I said, I don't know anything. I'm not even sure if the dude is the one who got her because, from what I hear from the street, he got popped a couple of years back. But rest damn sure if yaw finds Black before me, yaw going to have a new case to solve." Gunner was slick and quick; he knew giving them a false name would buy him some time.

"Did you say Black?"

"Yeah, that's the dude's name who I owed dough to. But I'm telling you. The nigga is a ghost." The police wrote down black on his pad.

"We have far better resources. Thank you, and if you think of something else, call the woman's family or us. It's the least you can do." Gunner nodded in agreeance as the officers let themselves out.

Eighteen

"**M**rs. Jackson, you need to slip into this gown."

"Mrs. Jackson, you need to sign right here before we begin.

"Mrs. Jackson, have you considered all of the mental and physical repercussions of this?"

"Mrs. Jackson, this won't hurt a bit."

"Mrs. Jackson, wake up. Congratulations! You just killed an innocent baby."

"Mrs. Jackson, how could you, a grown woman, be so careless!"

"Mrs. Jackson, how would you like to have a look at the dead fetus, you bitch!"

"Mrs. Jackson! Turn over and look at the life you just destroyed!"

####

Sitting up ramrod straight in her bed, Paris could feel the sweat pouring down her temples. The voices always started so kindly, gently, and caring. Before long, they always turned malicious and patronizing, like a million collective demon voices from hell. They mocked her, charmed her, criticized her, and mugged her of sleep and sanity.

Paris began to hear them the moment the anesthetic wore off, and she found herself on a cold clinic bed, a rough white sheet covering her midsection. This had been going on for the past month. Her lack of sleep was beginning to affect her life, her daily routine, her parenting to baby Kash and her wife's duties to Kash. Not that she cared about neglecting Kash. He was part of the reason she had to make the decision to kill the one baby she had tried so hard to make. Paris went over the decision a million times in her head.

She badly wanted to tell Kash, but she was supposed to have been off pills for four months now. It was funny when she thought about it; Paris didn't know who to blame, her or Kash. Him for driving her to pills or her for taking them. She'd damaged their baby's health, and an abortion was the only option. Well, not the only option. She could choose to deliver a syndrome baby. This led her back to no option because Paris refused to bring a baby into this world to suffer a lifetime of pain and suffering. It was a cold world just being born normal.

####

"Hey, baby," Kash called out cheerfully as he walked through the swinging doors to their kitchen.

"Hey, Kash," Paris pasted on a fake smile and said as she leaned over the counter, chopping garlic as though she were killing an enemy.

"Did you remember the basil?"

"Yelp, I got it right here... I think the only place that has fresh basil this time of the year is the Curb Market, and you know I wasn't driving across the city just for basil. So, instead, I got a bottle of the dried kind," Kash said as he walked toward the counter to set the plastic grocery bags down. Kash's real problem was missing the game. He hated missing even a second of any football or basketball game. He was worse than a woman who needed to watch her soap opera or reality show.

"You did what?" Paris snapped as she flung the knife on the floor. It landed inches from Kash's right foot.

"I asked you something simple."

"Paris, you are tripping. Watch that shit." Kash replied seriously as he slowly stepped back toward the door.

"I asked you one simple fucking favor, and you couldn't even do that right," Paris yelled like an angry black woman as she flipped the cutting board of garlic onto the floor.

"What is your fucking excuse? I asked for basil, and you brought me some dried shit. After all, I have done for you, was that too much to ask?" she screamed through her tears. She was clearly angry about something, but Kash knew it couldn't be the basil. He was so in shock at her language and the tone she used; he didn't even feel the groceries slip out of his hands and fall to the floor. Looking at Paris crumpled to the floor in tears, he felt helpless and guilty.

He had to go get Stephanie; in all his years with Paris, he had never seen her act this way. He didn't know what was going on.

"Baby, I didn't think it was that serious. But look, I am going. I'm leaving now. I am gonna find you some fresh basil even if it kills me."

"No! Don't fucking bother! You can't do anything right! Fuck this!" Paris yelled as she began bawling. As Paris backed against the wall, the kitchen door swung open. Like a miracle on Christmas, it was Stephanie with Baby Kash. Confused, she looked as Paris reached up for a terra-cotta soup tureen. Turning to Kash, she looked down and read the fear on his face.

"What the hell is going on? Kash? What did you do to her?" she said hurriedly.

"I bought dried basil," Kash replied in his zombie-like tone.

"You bought dried basil," Stephanie repeated.

"Yes, and she went off on me like a loaded pistol," Kash told her in a pain-stricken voice as she reached out for baby Kash.

"Paris, what is your problem?" Stephanie asked as she took a few steps forward.

"Are you upset about something? Are you on your period?"

"Momma, this has nothing to do with a period!" she yelled. "My fucking world is falling apart, and you ask me about a period? I'm fucking married to an asshole! I fucking hate my life right now!" Taking the soup tureen, she lifted it above her head.

"Paris. We bought that in Cozumel. It cost a fortune. You didn't even want to put anything in it, and now you want to break it? Put it down, baby. Tell me what's wrong."

"You're such a motherfucking bitch the only thing you can fucking think about is how much shit costs. Fuck you!" Paris snapped as she threw the tureen at Kash. He ducked just in a nick of time before it crashed against the wall.

"Hold up!" Kash yelled, raising his voice several octaves.

"I will not let you break shit and berate me in my house, no matter how mad you are!"

"Your house? Motherfucker, may I remind you that we are married. This is our house, and I will throw and break my share of shit if I choose to. Fuck you!" she said as she flung a blender against the steel refrigerator door.

A dark, angry, stormy cloud covered Kash's face. He wanted to hit Paris. Hitting her so hard that she would think twice before disrespecting him again. Instead, he leaned against the wall and drew in a breath of courage. Turning, he addressed Stephanie, who stood frozen in place.

"Take Kash Jr. into his bedroom."

"Kash, I can't leave her like this."

"Stephanie, take my son into his room right now," he repeated, punctuating every word.

"Please."

"But Kash..." Stephanie hesitated. Tears began to roll down her cheeks. At times like this, she despised being sick. She couldn't stand being so weak.

"Please, Stephanie." Stephanie stood there, still holding on to little Kash while he cried out loudly.

"Stephanie, standing there crying won't help her. Neither you nor Kash needs to see this," he said in a coaxingly soft voice.

"Hearing his tone, Stephanie spun around with little Kash on her hip and rushed toward the kitchen door.

"Thank you, Stephanie." Turning back towards Paris, he realized she was gathering up her purse.

"They don't have to go. I'm leaving. I need some time for myself. I need to get my head right. Don't worry, I'll be fine. Don't call me, please. I need to do this for me. I don't want to hear from you, Kash. Or no one, for that matter."

"What's wrong?" Kash attempted to stop Paris from exiting the kitchen, but she pushed right past him.

"Just don't call me. Give me time, and I'll tell you later." Kash stood frozen and confused in the middle of the living room where he had chased Paris to. He figured giving her space like she asked to keep from throwing gasoline on flames was best.

Nineteen

The rugged sounds of four-wheelers engines echoed as Omari, Rasheed, and a crew of Rasheed's militants weaved through Rasheed's backyard, which was also the jungle. The girl Omari needed to see was just ahead, and it was deep in the wilderness, just outside of his mansion. When Rasheed said the girls were in his basement, that's what he thought he meant. Not in his backyard in the jungle.

"We are almost there! It's close," Rasheed yelled as he looked back at Omari, who was riding just a couple of yards behind him. Omari maneuvered the powerful machine as good as he could as he tried to keep up. Just as Omari grew tired, an open area appeared amid all the trees. It looked like a normal rest spot in the jungle. There were trees, monkeys, and exotic birds for the next hundreds of yards.

Rasheed and his goons stopped and got off their four-wheelers. Omari slowed to a stop and looked around in confusion.

"Why did we stop? Are we lost?" Omari asked as he turned off his ignition and stepped off the bike.

"No, we are here," Rasheed said as he opened his arms and slowly spun around in the woods. *What the hell have I gotten myself into?* Omari thought as he suspiciously looked around.

"Follow me," Rasheed said as he waved over Omari. His goons mean mugged Omari as they gripped their assault riffles that hung by their shoulder straps. Nervously, Omari looked at Rasheed, who was walking away, and reluctantly followed him. Omari's heart began to pound; he didn't know what type of sick, twisted game Rasheed was playing with him. Rasheed stopped at a tree stump and then looked at Omari with a smile.

"Come on," Rasheed said as he reached down and grabbed what looked like a handle. Rasheed pulled it up, and a flight of stairs appeared, and Omari's eyes grew as big as cotton balls when he realized what it was. It was a secret passageway to an underground basement. He was blown away. Omari shook his head in disbelief and cracked a frown as he stepped down, and Rasheed followed close behind.

The squeaky wood stairs led about thirteen feet underground and opened to a spacious vault set up like a shelter. Young girls from the ages of ten to twenty-seven were scattered around everywhere. Some were cooking, breastfeeding, doing hair, sleeping, and they were all half-naked. With large ugly goon men hanging around, guarding the exit while enjoying the view of the young girls.

"This is where my money is made. We produce some of the best-looking babies in the world! This is where some of the richest women worldwide shop for their babies." Being a doctor in Africa, Omari had seen some of the most stomach-turning things, and never did he get weak, but seeing the young girls slave to Rasheed and his militants disgusted him. Sex escapades were going on in different rooms, and neither of the girls seemed to be enjoying themselves, of course.

"Do you see why I needed to trust you before exposing you to my Jordan box?" Rasheed talked about his operation like it was legit, and he saw no wrong in what he was doing to the ladies.

"Yes... I see why." Omari stuttered.

"Now, you're welcome to help yourself, but any and every creation belongs to me. That's unless you want to buy you a woman to take home with you?" Rasheed tickled himself; he laughed hard as he jokily shoved Omari.

"Nawl, I'm good."

"Are you sure? I can give you a very good discount. And all my women are trained. You don't have to worry about them being any trouble." Omari could barely breathe, and it wasn't anything wrong with the oxygen in the room. He just couldn't believe his ears. It was Africans like Rasheed that gave the African culture such a bad name.

"Let's go to the back so I can introduce you to Honey," Rasheed said. They walked through the passage to a steel door at the end. An armed man that was as black as tar with shades on stood posted.

"I need to see Honey," Rasheed said as he approached the man. The guard opened the door and stepped to the side. Rasheed walked in, and Omari followed closely behind. A chiseled man sat in a chair while two of the thickest ladies Omari had ever seen nursed Honey. She is flat on a hospital bed, inhaling and exhaling deep breaths.

"How long has she been in pain?" Omari asked as he rushed over to the bed.

"For about four hours now," one of the beautiful women answered.

"Now, I need you to take care of her, Omari. She's one of my best creators. Her kids sell like hotcakes." Omari assumed she was an expensive piece of cake since she was lighter than the other girls. Her eyes were emerald green, and her skin was smooth like silk. She was indeed the most beautiful woman he had ever seen.

"How old is she?" Omari looked back to ask Rasheed.

"She's seventeen." He bragged.

"How many kids does she have?" None of this mattered at the moment; Omari was just curious.

"She's had four. This will be her fifth child." Omari could wring Rasheed's neck, but he knew soon after he would be dead.

"Please, help me. It hurts really bad." Honey gripped Omari's fresh white t-shirt and said.

"Where is the pain, Honey?"

"It's everywhere. This doesn't feel the same. Something is not right!" Honey cried out between deep breaths.

"When was the last time she had proper medical treatment?" Omari yelled back to Rasheed as he softly pressed down on her stomach. The two men who guarded Honey began to speak in their native tongue while Omari watched, unsure of what was being said. They were going back and forth about something, and Omari was dying to know what the topic of discussion was. After a couple of minutes, Omari stood tall, displaying his six-foot-three frame, then walked over to Rasheed and said, "Listen, I don't work under these conditions. I need to know her health history before I can do anything. I'm not trying to wear death on my hands." Rasheed shook his head slowly as the two guards continued to discuss.

"She doesn't look good." Omari leaned in to whisper into Rasheed's ear.

"I got to know what has happened to her for me to help her." Rasheed didn't blink as Omari continued to whisper into his ear.

"Honey! Point out the person who did it, now!" Rasheed broke his silence to say with a mug so sharp it could slice a finger. Slowly, Honey lifted her finger to point out the biggest guard. His gold teeth shun bright, and his bald head dripped in sweat.

"Rasheed... Listen!" he tried to explain.

"Did what? What did he do?" Omari snapped before he rushed back over to Honey's side.

"Listen, you just hold tight. I'm going to deliver your baby, and I promise you if you do as I say, you will make it. I need some privacy; everybody out!" Rasheed didn't hesitate; he followed Omari's orders as if he was running things. The girls stayed behind to assist Omari as Rasheed signaled the men to follow him out. As soon as they left the room, Omari heard a loud sound. He was sure it was the rifle going off. He ran to the door, and sure enough, Rasheed had killed the guard Honey pointed out. He lay still in his fresh blood outside the door.

"If she dies, so do you," Rasheed said to the next guard that helped guard Honey's room. Stunned at Rasheed's actions, Omari slowly walked back into the room to tend to Honey. After hours of complications and pain Honey delivered a beautiful baby boy. She was thankful for Omari's help. She feared for her life, but as he promised, everything was okay. She begged him to let her repay him, but he refused and told her she shouldn't be touched sexually for at least three months. She had never met a man so caring and beautiful in all her days. She had been with Rasheed since she was nine, and not once had she seen a man like Omari come through the vault. He was beautiful internally and externally.

Omari made Rasheed promise that he would give Honey a three-month bed rest, and he did. He assured Omari his word was worth more than gold and that Honey wouldn't be touched for three months. He also assured Omari that she would be catered to until she could get back on her feet.

Twenty

Hours passed as London and Jordan shared laughs, cries, and heart-to-heart conversations, while Rasheed and Omari discussed business over D'usse Cognac. The purpose of the trip was different for Jordan than for Omari. He came on business, but she wanted to get a feel of Africa. She wanted to mingle with the African people. She had never been outside of Georgia, and this trip was such an experience for her.

She immediately connected with her when she found out London was from Atlanta. She was still a little clueless about how London met Rasheed, but she didn't bother asking again when she noticed London changing the subject. In fact, every time Jordan had asked London something personal - if she had kids, how she and Rasheed met, was planning to go back to Atlanta, if she had siblings--- she would direct the conversation focus point back to Jordan.

"So, where are the cool spots in Africa? I want to see more. Omari has been working non-stop since we got here, and I haven't had a chance to really do anything." Jordan said as she sipped on the ice-cold lemonade Kenya had prepared for them.

"Really, girl? You haven't done anything?" London asked.

"No, nothing interesting." London teased her luminous curls, then smeared her lip gloss around her lips before jumping up from her seat.

"Watch me work." She said before prancing over to the men who carried on a full conversation about Africa's natural resources and how the world stole from them.

"Rasheed, baby?" London said in her sexy voice, knowing she would get a smirk or even a full smile out of Rasheed. He laughed when she talked sweetly to him, only because she hardly ever spoke to him at all.

"Yes, love." He turned around to say with his smile reaching from one ear to another.

"I was wondering if I could take Jordan to see some of Africa. She hasn't seen much since she got here because you've been working with her husband non-stop." London twirled around in her colorful sundress biting down on her bottom lip as Rasheed thought about his answer.

"Nothing major; we might just do a little shopping in the villages or something like that." Rasheed looked at Omari; Omari looked at Rasheed, and then they both looked back at London.

"Okay, fine. You girls can go run around Africa." Rasheed knew without a doubt he was being played, but he didn't care; he'll take anything London was dishing out. She had made him feel like a man, and nothing could beat that feeling.

"Let's go spend some money, girl." Jordan couldn't believe how much the women in Africa submitted to their men. She would have never asked Omari if she could go anywhere, but she assumed *maybe this is how it works over here.* Little did she know, London was far from the submissive type. She was just making the best of the hand she was dealt.

Being in Africa gave Jordan a peace that she had never felt before. Africa had been painted as such an ugly place back home that she had no idea it would be the complete opposite. The last time she had seen Africa on TV back home, they were talking about help donated to a group of kids who seemed to be dying from starvation. But in person, it was a completely different picture. The community of people that lived there seemed to be so happy.

"The energy here is so contagious." Jordan said as she looked around, smiling, feeling complete as she took it all in.

"They rebuilt this village nicely, and of course, it's run by Rasheed now. He donates money and goods to this community, but of course, it's never for free." Kenya said.

"How long have you been in Africa?" Jordan asked Kenya.

"Oh, my whole life. This is home for me." Kenya answered proudly. The three girls held hands as they walked through the village, and it seemed as if they were family.

"This must have been a ball growing up here?" Growing up in the States had taken away Jordan's appreciation for nature, for community, and for simplicity. She was wooed by labels, wealth, and the hustle, but as she became acquainted with her roots, she realized that none of that mattered.

"I could stay here forever." Jordan said.

"Then stay Jordan. You are enslaving yourself by living in fear. You're free to do whatever it is your heart desire. Do what you want to do," Kenya said. "Who would your decision displease? Omari?"

"No, he's from here. He probably wouldn't mind, but then again, he has fallen in love with America."

"Once an African man, always an African man. He wouldn't mind." Kenya interrupted.

"He has both the city sway and the rugged nature. And he can have that here. Besides, I think he would do whatever it takes to make you happy. That man seems to adore you." Jordan inhaled a deep breath and then exhaled. It felt good to have someone to love her unconditionally because, for a while, Shawn had her feeling like love was just a word and that the real thing didn't exist.

"I think my heart's linked to too many peoples in the States for me to commit to such a big move, but just thinking about it does bring me joy."

London drifted ahead of Kenya and Jordan. All this staying in Africa permanently got her feeling down. She badly wanted to yell to Jordan, *hell, you can have my place. I'll give my right arm to leave this place. It's not that damn beautiful.* To ease her rattling nerves, London purchased crafts from the locals and trinkets from the children. She didn't need any of the stuff, but she knew what she spent on homemade trinkets could help feed a family for a week. And that always made her feel better.

The locals were out hustling, but she wondered what her life would be like if Rasheed wasn't a wealthy African that kidnapped her. *What if he was a broke gangster raping her every night.* Life could be much worse, she concluded as she made her way through the village.

"My village is just a few blocks from here." Before Kenya could say another word, London already knew where this conversation was heading. Kenya wanted to take a trip home.

"London, could we just take a quick trip to my village, please?" Jordan didn't get why Kenya had to beg London for permission to visit her home, but then again, it was a lot of things that Jordan didn't get about the African culture.

"Sure, we can check it out. But we can't stay long. Rasheed will start to worry if we don't make it back in decent time." London said as she and Jordan followed Kenya through the village.

On a quest to find Kenya's family, they went about the village asking questions to see if they could find any leads. Nobody knew who Kenya was or her family. They inquired about them to anyone they saw, but it was to no avail. Kenya began to get discouraged. The village had changed drastically, and everybody Kenya knew was dead. Rasheed had ruined their village. She badly wanted to cry, but she fought back her tears. She didn't feel like being weak. Although she knew it was a long shot, something deep inside told her that if she came back that her baby sister Sahara would be there waiting for her. They were losing sunlight, and Kenya knew they had to be heading back, so she called off the search.

"Thank yaw for helping me. They're gone; we're not going to find them; let's just go back."

"Come on, we can just keep looking." Jordan said, not understanding the consequences if they returned past the curfew.

"London, you don't mind, do you?" Jordan turned and asked London.

"It's not up to me, honey. Trust me," London replied.

"What? Yaw got to ask Rasheed about this too?" Jordan knew only what Omari had told her about London's situation, but from the looks of things, she had started to believe that maybe London was here willingly and enjoying the high life.

"Yes, in fact, it is! I'm not trying to get her hurt again, trying to save me." Kenya snapped.

"Now, let's just go before I get us all in trouble." Jordan picked her face up off the ground and followed behind Kenya and London. She had felt stupid for butting into their business. How dare she question their set-up. Who knows what they've gone through.

"Kenya!" The three girls all turned their heads at the loud echoing voice coming from behind them.

"Zoya!" Kenya yelled back when she realized that it was her little cousin calling out her name.

"Wait up!" Zoya yelled out as she ran full speed towards Kenya.

"Oh my God, I can't believe it's really you. We didn't know what had happened to you." Zoya kneeled on her knees to catch her breath.

"Oh, my goodness, Zoya, where is everybody?" The two hugged each other tight, kissing one another on the cheeks.

"Well, Grandma Eartha died when Rasheed boys took Sahara." Kenya teared up immediately. Her grandmother was dead, and her baby sister was also caught up with the same monster she was entangled with.

"You mean to tell me Rasheed has her sister too?" London said.

114

"And who is miss thing?" Zoya snapped.

"This is London, the queen. Rasheed's wife."

"You mean to tell me that you are friends with his wife? The man who has ruined our lives forever!" Kenya quickly placed her hand over Zoya's mouth.

"Are you trying to get me killed or something," Kenya whispered as she squeezed Zoya's mouth closed tight with her hand.

"I'm sorry," she murmured through Kenya's hand.

"This lady has practically given her life up for me. She's been nothing less than great to me. Trust me, it's not what you think. She's a victim too." Hearing Kenya explain things to Zoya made Jordan feel stupid all over again. All the glitz and glamour made her forget. London was the victim. She seemed to be having a perfect life but deep down, she was most likely, just as hurt as her twin sister.

"I'll check and see if I can find Sahara. Don't move, Zoya; I'm going to try to come back and check on you. So, we can catch up, but I got to go. If not, he won't trust us out again." Zoya and Kenya hugged each other once more, and then London, Jordan, and Kenya rushed through the crowd of people to pretend they were looking for Tony, the guard that they purposely ditched.

Twenty-One

Just when Omari was about to wander the mansion to find London, a group of beautiful women burst through the private room where he had just delivered his last baby. They were more beautiful than the girls flaunted around in the hip-hop videos. Melanin was an understatement; these girls' skin glowed effortlessly. Some were as dark as Hershey, and some skin was as smooth as caramel, but none of them had fair skin. Just beautiful black women dressed as if they were going to a festival in Barbados.

The very courageous one fetched Omari and grabbed him by the hand. She was dark as chocolate with autumn red hair. Her makeup was flawless; it was as if she didn't have any on. Omari was confused. He didn't understand what was going on. His mouth hung open like a kid in a candy store. *What is this man up to now?* He thought as she pulled him out of the room towards the party. Behind her trailed a mass of gold and black balloons; engraved words read, *'Thank you for your services.'* Omari spied the women's beautiful shapes, and immediately, he felt guilty for looking. The Jordan was the apple of his eye. He had no business looking at the girls' nicely rounded asses. Some of their asses were beyond large, at least twice the size of Jordan. They bounced like tight basketball, never wiggling out of place. Omari tried to shake the images away as they pulled him deeper into the crowd. But as soon as he spotted Jordan clapping for his arrival, all his guilt melted away.

"Surprise!" the party of people screamed out to him.

"What is this?" he questioned as the ladies set him down in the best spot for the show, in the middle of the seating area.

"This is your celebration, my man. I know today is your last day working with me, so I wanted to send you home in style." Rasheed said as he stretched his arms out wide like a king bragging about his throne.

"Oh, you didn't have to do this, my man." Omari attempted to rise from the seat, but Rasheed pushed him down.

"Oh, no. I insist." The beautiful girls began to entertain Omari with a routine African dance. Both Omari and Jordan were entertained; it was a sight to see. The celebration was a success, and everyone was a little more hyped up than they should be. The guards were even enjoying themselves; not once did they have to squeeze tight to their guns. Omari's eyes scoped out the scene like a hawk on prey, he had a mission, and he had to keep focus.

"London, dance with me." Omari grabbed London and took her to the dance floor. It was nothing strange but very planned. Omari had given Jordan the instructions to dance with Rasheed, so his dancing with London didn't seem suspicious. Purposely, Jordan gave Rasheed the dance of his life. All eyes were fixated on her as she moved her body like a snake feeling supercharged. Rasheed enjoyed every minute of the attention. And the view was nice too. Everything about the flowing silk dress she had on the screamed goddess. Her feet were moving with grace, and her heart was beating with fear as she watched Omari fill London in on their plan.

"Listen, don't look down, but I just slipped something in your bra. I need you to have Kenya drop two drops of it in the bodyguard's drinks and three into Rasheed's." London was confused but attentive.

"What are you talking about?" She asked before sipping low in front of him like she was more into his moves than his conversation.

"I know who you are, London. I know your twin sister, Paris's husband, Kash, personally." London's heart dropped to her knees. It took every muscle in her body to fight back her tears. Who would have known? She thought.

"I'm here undercover. I'm going to help you get out of here. The medicine will knock the guards out, and as soon as you see the coast is clear, I'm going to need you to make a run for it. Run straight through the jungle; there will be soldiers waiting for you there." London couldn't believe her ears. She had given up on hope. She had failed at running away so many times that she almost didn't want to attempt again.

"Are you sure this is going to work?" She asked right before Omari dipped her.

"No, I'm not sure, but what other choice do you have?" London thought long as the two tangled around the floor, and Omari was right. What other choice did she have?

"Jordan and I are about to leave, but we won't be far. We'll be in the woods waiting on you. The best time to do this is now because the party is dying down. It'll take less than twenty minutes to put them out, and as soon as they are out cold, you run." Just the thought of running made London's palms sweaty. Her heartbeat increased drastically, and her gut felt as if it would explode and a rainbow of butterflies would just fly out.

"London?" Omari said to snap her back to reality.

"You got this; we have American soldiers on our side."

"Okay, I'm going to do it. Please, don't leave me. I'll be out there, even if it kills me."

"No one is going to get killed, just do as I said, and everything will be all right."

"Just don't leave me." Omari looked into London's glistening hazel eyes and replied, "I won't, I promise."

####

The crowd had died down, and Kenya did just as she was instructed. Every guard had a drop of Omari's potion dripped into their champagne, cognac, or wine. Whatever they were drinking. Kenya had loaded them up, but it was past thirty minutes later, and no one had fallen yet. Both London and Kenya had begun to worry.

"What if it didn't work?" Kenya whispered as she poured London a drink.

"It's going to work if you do as I asked you," London whispered with a mean mug on her face. Kenya started thinking, *maybe I should have put two drips like she said instead of three, dammit.*

"Baby, can I have this dance?" The harsh scent of cognac rushed through London's nostrils as Rasheed grabbed her by the hand. He was drunk; he knew it, she knew it, and so did everybody else. They could see him struggling to keep it together. It was like some sort of out-of-body experience. His legs did not work as he told them. Neither did his hands that kept gripping London's ass.

Deep inside, his brain was signaling him to sit down. But his body wasn't listening. Rasheed could feel himself moving, his body was doing what it wanted, but he wanted to sit down. He was suddenly feeling dizzy, and London took notice. A few more two steps and suddenly, it all went dark. He's drunk, out cold. Laid out, flat onto the floor. The guards looked upon him with laughter in their eyes. They knew he was drunk, and so were they. And boom, before you knew it, everyone was falling out. It was like a contagious disease had hit the air and affected everyone rapidly.

"Oh, my God! It worked." Kenya screamed out as she looked around at a mansion full of sleepy armed men.

"Shhh!" London said as she bent down to check to see if Rasheed could hear her.

"Rasheed? She called out quietly.

"It worked," London quickly jumped up and ran to get baby Hope. Behind her was Kenya.

"What do I do now?" Kenya asked as soon as they reached baby Hope's nursery.

"You go to go to the basement and find your sister." London doubled back around.

"Oh wait, there are armed men there. Don't do that." Kenya paced the floor, and so did London as they tried to think.

"I'll figure something out. I still have a lot of the potion left." London's heart wanted to cry for Kenya. She couldn't stand the thought of leaving her, but this was her only chance shot at freedom. She grabbed the bag she had pre-packed for years out of the secret safe she had in Hope's room.

"Kenya, I'm so sorry." Tears dripped from London's eyes like a running faucet. The two hugged each other for long minutes tight like they were sisters from the same mother.

"I know you have to do what you have to do. I'm so thankful for you, London. I'll never forget you." Kenya managed to croak out with a knot in her throat.

"I'm going to try and send you help. Just hold tight, okay."

"Okay,"

"I have to go now," Before disappearing out the door, London turned back to say, "And I'll never forget you either, little sister." London's words ate Kenya more than she would ever know. For one, Kenya secretly crushed on London, and she desired to be more than a little sister. Secondly, knowing she'll always remember her but never being in her life as a friend or lover hurt worse than a bullet wound she imagined.

"Bye, London," Kenya said before London dashed out of the room, down the stairs, out of the house, and into the woods with baby Hope on her hip.

Cutting their way through the dense, suffocating jungle, London and Baby Hope ran for their lives. Trees tall as cathedrals surrounded them, and every view was uniquely dark. London didn't know where she was running to; she just ran. Unlike most, she had trouble breathing in the fresh air. Though her lungs kept heaving air in and out, it was more like drowning than breathing for the girl who was raised on the east coast of America.

The jungle seemed to have an intelligence of its own. Its voices were the sudden screech of a parrot, the flicker of a monkey swinging through the branches overhead, and every sound; London thought it was Rasheed and his goons coming for her. She sped up, dashing through the trees like Tarzan. And then, twenty minutes deep into the woods, a strange white light- almost holy- shimmered through the path of trees.

"London?" Omari called out as she ran full speed towards her.

"Omari!" she yelled back, running like Forest towards him.

"Oh, my goodness, you waited for me." As soon as London was in Omari's arms, she broke down into sobbing. She cried like a baby. She was so weak she couldn't take the few steps she needed to board the helicopter.

"Come on, London, let's get you out of here." Omari grabbed baby Hope, and the buff American Soldier that ran with Omari to meet London halfway swooped London off her feet. Her body hung over his shoulders as they ran back to the helicopter.

"There are some girls back there that need you guys' help. They're all kids." London cried out as the American soldier scrapped her into a seat belt.

"Don't worry, London, they're fully aware of the operation. The men already have men in place to raid the house. The girls will be rescued. We just had to get you out of the house first since you are an American citizen." London had never been so proud of her country as she was right now. At this very moment, she was thankful for all the men and women who fought for the country. Memorial Day had a new meaning.

"Thank you, guys, so much."

Jordan wiped away her tears as they lifted off into the air.

Twenty-Two

hree days passed as Jordan and London shared laughs, cries, and heart-to-heart conversations, over good ole New Orleans cuisine. They were only supposed to be in New Orleans for a couple of days until Omari got confirmation that Rasheed was caught and put away for good. But a couple of days changed on the day they were scheduled to return to Atlanta. Omari stood in the kitchen on his cell phone, talking to his connect in Africa, and London accidentally overheard bits of the conversation.

"So, he isn't captured yet?" Omari asked. He paced back and forth as he tried to figure out their next move. Every day, London asked him when they could go home and if Rasheed had been prisoned, and every day he told her the same thing, *not yet, but they'll catch him before it's time for us to leave New Orleans*. It was time for them to leave, and Rasheed hadn't been caught. Omari knew he had to come up with a believable explanation and quick. There was no way they could return to Atlanta with Rasheed still on the loose. It just wasn't smart. Going to Atlanta right away would be too risky and predictable. It was the main reason they chose to hide out in New Orleans. The location had no connections to either London or Omari.

"Omari, man, just sit tight. I'll give you some good news soon. Trust me, we not letting up on this motha-fucka. He not going to get away with this shit. That's my word." Omari listened, staring in a daze. It wasn't him that was having a problem with sitting tight but London.

"Aight, man, ensure you get at me as soon as you know something. You know I got two anxious women on my nerves. They're going to want to know something very soon."

"Cool. I got you. Oh, and before you go. You can let the women know that the girls are safe. They're all receiving proper medical treatment and will be returned to their families soon." Omari face lit up. He had something good to tell London, plus he had been praying daily that they would be able to rescue all the girls after getting word that some of Rasheed's goons hid some of the girls in the woods.

"Okay, that's great to hear, man. That's damn good news. Keep in touch, and let me know something as soon as you know." Omari said just before he pushed the END button worriedly. He had been stalling London for hours, trying to distract her from the truth; Rasheed hadn't been captured. He had been scooped up by one of the guards who was absent from the party due to a bowel movement. They fled the scene, and the soldiers hadn't been able to locate them.

Omari thought about lying to London, but he concluded that it would only worsen things when she found out the truth. The last thing a woman like London needed was to be lied to. She had been around enough snakes in her life.

"So, what's going on?" London's voice startled Omari. He jumped a little, then placed his cell phone in his back pocket.

"We'll be able to make the Mardi Gras festivities after all!" He said loudly with a contagious smile. Hoping his words traveled to the sitting area where Jordan was.

"Really, baby, we can stay?" Jordan shouted before she jumped up from the sofa.

"Yes, we can stay a little while longer. You know, just until the festivities are over, though." Jordan hugged Omari like he was her long-lost friend.

"Good, because I've always wanted to come to New Orleans during Mardi Gras." *You always wanted to do everything*, London thought as she stood irritably with her arms folded.

"Girl, you really haven't been outside of Atlanta, have you?"

"Girl, no, I could never afford to go anywhere; between raising my niece, Destiny, and having to maintain my bills, a sistah never could manage to save enough coins."

"Well, that's alright, baby. You got me now, and we're going to do so much traveling you're going to forget where you live." Omari's corny, unfunny joke made London laugh. Omari and Jordan were compatible. They were made for each other.

"So, Omari, what was the good news I heard you cheering about?" Omari clapped, snapped, then pointed his two index fingers at London, "We'll talk about it over dinner. Get dressed, ladies; we're going to watch the parade from one of the best restaurants in town, Court of two sisters." London was no fool. She could tell Omari was hiding something. His craving to spoil them was a dead giveaway. Jordan didn't notice, but why would she. She was having the time of her life. Meanwhile, London was anxious to see how her life was about to turn out.

####

The costumes were as colorful as a London garden. Bold yellows, magenta, cyan, and emerald green sequins were sparkling in the brilliant afternoon sun, and feathers of every color. Wherever you looked, there were painted faces and masks; the stilt walkers marched down the middle of the crowd blowing bubbles or waving as they went along. The jazz music was the heartbeat of the crowd, and they swayed long limbs in time to the beat. The Jordan had never seen anything like it. Girls were flashing their boobs for ju-ju beads, and the people were energetic and joyful.

"I just love the spirit of the people here," Jordan said as she sipped on her homemade iced tea.

"I think I'm more in love with the food," London said as she stuffed her mouth with a fried alligator.

124

"I can't believe you're eating that?" Jordan frowned as London stuffed more of the alligator into her mouth.

"You just don't know good food, girl," Omari responded as he stuffed his mouth with a fish that looked him in the eyes as he cut it thin.

"Yaw, just nasty. I'm not eating none of that mess. I'll stick to the gumbo and shrimp." Both Omari and London laughed as they continued to stuff their mouths, watching the live festivities outside.

"I want to go out there."

"Yaw can go; I'll watch the girls for yaw." Omari turned to Jordan to say as he wiped his mouth clean with a napkin.

"So, Omari, about the phone call?" London said, changing the subject.

"Yes, about that phone call." Omari began to sweat bullets. London could tell he was more nervous than a college student at a first interview for their dream job.

"I'm a big girl, Omari; I can handle it," London said, hoping to release Omari's stress.

"It's not that, London; I just don't want to sway your thoughts in the wrong direction. I have nothing bad to tell you; I just don't have nothing great to tell you, either. Oh, wait, well, I do have something good to tell you." Both London and Jordan watched anxiously.

"How about you tell me the not-so-good first," London demanded.

"Okay. Rasheed hasn't been caught yet, and we're going to have to stay in New Orleans a little longer." London took a deep breath, and then she exhaled. She knew she should be patient, considering she's been this long without her family, but she really couldn't fight the urge. It was like the closer she got to reuniting with Paris, Stephanie, and her son, the more impatient she grew.

"Okay. I'll just have to wait. There's really nothing we can do."

"I'm sorry, London."

"Oh, you have nothing to be sorry about, Omari. You and Jordan have been nothing less than great to me, and I'm forever grateful." London's eyes glistened as her voice began to crack.

"I'm just going have to be patient, that's all," London said.

"On the sunny side of things, all the girls were captured, and they're receiving medical treatment as we speak, and then they'll all be returned to their families." Knowing Kenya would be united with her family brought joy to London's heart. She smiled, mumbling, "Thank you, God. Thank you."

"Now, let's make the best of a worrisome situation." Jordan said.

"Let's go party, girl!" London burst into laughter. The Jordan was just full of good energy. The Mardi Gras had really gotten to her.

"Okay, you crazy chic. Now, are you sure you got both of them?" London asked Omari with an unsure mug.

"I got them. Go ahead, have some fun. Live a little and keep your boobs in your bras, ladies." London and Jordan giggled at Omari on their way out the door.

"Bye, Omari, don't wait up!" Jordan yelled back.

Twenty-Three

It was as if God had adjusted the colors of Stephanie's subdivision over the years. Everything was brighter than it should be; the trees were not just green but radiant virescent hues. The houses in the neighborhood had been repainted by the moonlight and now stood vibrant in the golden rays that fell unfettered through the clear sky. The road that should be grey was a sleek river of black with perfectly painted lines, and the street lamps were blue. But they had never been blue, not ever. Everything was so right that it was wrong, really wrong.

The front yards that had been ruffled with the weakness of late Paris was a riot of colorful blooms. London turned back to look at her mother's house, and the curtain twitched! Someone was there. She hurried to the front door only to find it was locked. She banged on the door, and a face appeared at the window... Her face... Only it wasn't her face; it was Paris's. She screamed out for help as one of Rasheed's goons scooped her up into his arm. "Help me!" Paris screamed out, only London couldn't touch her. She was too far away. London was stuck in position; no matter how hard she tried, she couldn't move. The dream had her locked as if she was in a sunken place. London shook her head mutely. She'd been having the same dream for hours. She breathed in and out hard. Finally, she realized it wasn't real. Quickly, she sat straight up in bed; her body shivered as if she was naked. She wiped the dripping sweat from her forehead as she heaved in and out loudly. The nightmare had shaken her nerves. Rasheed didn't know she was a twin, and the last thing she needed was him mistaking Paris for her. She couldn't live with herself knowing Paris had to suffer the consequences of her action.

Loudly, baby Hope broke into sobbing. She had scared the nightmare quivers out of London, and just like that, she was back to reality. Omari and Jordan barged into the room before she could jump up to Hope's rescue.

"Are you okay, London?" Jordan rushed to her side to ask.

"Yes, I'm fine." Omari looked around the room. Checking behind the window curtains and the closet doors.

"I'm you guys; it was just another bad dream. I keep dreaming Rasheed is going to get Paris instead of me." London lifted Hope in her arms and held on to her tightly.

"It's okay little momma; I got you." She said as she rocked Hope into comfort.

"I'm sorry for waking yaw. Did I wake up, baby Journey?"

"Naw, that baby sleeps through anything when she's on that Tylenol." Jordan joked as she and Omari made their way out the door.

"We just one room over; holla if you need us," Jordan said.

"Okay, I will."

####

London sat on the edge of a bench outside an old white neglected house, her eyes trained keenly on the path to the door for Jordan's six-inch Louboutin heels. It was odd for her to make a connection so fast and give her trust so easily, tentatively though it was. There was something in the way Jordan smiled, a warmth, a genuineness, a softness of spirit. London just couldn't pass up vibing with a person with such good energy.

Jordan listened to London whenever she spoke like she was absorbing her words, not simply getting her "turn" over and done with so she could return to some other topic. The more time London spent with Jordan, the more her spirit lifted; she was the new friend London needed for so long. The opposite of Egypt. After thirty long seconds, Jordan appeared with a large smile on her face.

"Now, do you promise to keep an open mind?" Jordan said to London as she approached the bench

"Oh lord, what have you gotten me into?" London said before she rose from the bench.

"It's something I always wanted to do." London investigated Jordan's sparkling eyes, knowing she couldn't turn back now. She was too excited about this surprise she had gone against her husband for.

"Is this something you and your hubby had an altercation about earlier?" London asked as she followed Jordan into the house.

"Yes."

"But you said you wouldn't do it?" London said.

"Yeah, I know. I lied. Shoot me." Jordan led London deeper into the mysterious dark house...

"Hey, ladies." The old WAG with grey butt-length dreads spoke softly, flipping through her reading cards.

"Oh, hell naw, Jordan! You done brought me to physic?" Jordan pulled on London's arm, pulling her back into the room.

"You promised you would keep an open mind," Jordan said.

"Yeah, but not this shit, Jordan. I don't need this in my life right now." Jordan continued to pull London deeper into the room, and finally, after ten seconds of scuffling, London willingly walked to the table.

"To be honest, I don't even believe in this stuff," London said as she took a seat at the table with her brows creased and face tense. When Jordan sat, wine in hand, she asked. "So how does this work?" her tone casual and light. The physics stared at her cards, "I don't know whether to start with the believer or non-believer?"

"That's it, I'm out of here." London jumped up from her seat, heading for the door.

"Afia says, *thank you for taking care of baby Hope.*" London froze in her steps. She couldn't believe her ears. How could this lady know Afia or baby Hope?

"Jordan, what you have been doing, sitting in here telling this lady all of my damn business?" London snapped.

"No, I swear. I haven't told her anything. I just came to see if she could fit us in her schedule because I was told she doesn't do walk-ins." Jordan's words rattled as she spoke. She could tell London was furious, and she didn't want her to think she would betray her.

"Paris forgives you." The physic purposely added to assure London that Jordan had nothing to do with her knowledge. London hadn't told Jordan about her betrayal of Paris, so she knew Jordan was telling the truth about not saying anything to the stranger about her business. Tears streamed down London's beautiful hazel eyes.

"Come take a seat, London. I won't tell you nothing you don't want to hear. I promise." The elderly lady took a sip from her mug that was full of herbal tea and then continued, serious-faced. "I see; you've been through a great deal of things. What does your gut tell you about returning home? Why do you think you're having bad dreams, London?" Jordan grabbed on tightly to London's shimmering body.

"If you want to go, we can." Jordan said in an attempt to comfort London.

"Jordan, have you forgiven yourself for what you did to your best friend?" London's eyes widened as she looked suspiciously into Jordan's eyes.

"What did you do to your best friend?" London asked.

"Come sit down, ladies." Slowly and hesitantly, the ladies walked back over to the table and took a seat.

London's face crumpled again, "I don't know why I'm having the dreams or what my gut is telling me." For at least ten seconds, the room is silent. Both Jordan and London are very attentive.

"London, you've been through a lot, and soon you will see the rainbow, but before you do, you're going to catch a little more rain." Clara, the physic, grabbed London's hand, and again, the room went silent.

"Prepare yourself for shocking news." London's whole body shook. And her tears dripped silently. She knew Clara was telling nothing but the truth, and at that moment, she was glad Jordan pulled her into the house.

"Thank you." London managed to croak up. Clara didn't bother responding, but her head nod was all London needed.

"Jordan, Chyna's soul craves a genuine apology from you." Jordan broke down sobbing. Deep down, she knew she had hurt her best friend in the worse way, and never had she taken full responsibility for sleeping with her boyfriend.

"I'm so sorry, Chyna, I'm so sorry." Jordan cried out as her body rocked like a rocking chair. "She wants to hear those exact words from you, Jordan." London watched attentively as Jordan got her reading. Gently, Clara grabbed Jordan's hand and said, "You're going to be caught up in a love triangle. It's important that you follow your heart and not let your mind lead you." Jordan knew just what Clara was speaking of. Shawn had been calling her non-stop, trying to make nice. He had tried to express his love for her once when dropping baby Journey off, but she caught him off. It was a no-brainer; Clara was speaking about Omari and Shawn.

Clara made her face straighter than a poker player's and said, "Jordan, listen to your heart, not your mind." For a fraction of a second, the corners of Jordan's mouth twitched upward until her conscious mind asserted control again. Then Clara said, "You two women will eventually look back on this day and laugh. I see a fulfilling future for you too, but there will be lots of rain before that can happen." Clara's face was serious all the way from her eyes to her mouth, with no jokes in sight. Slowly, she let go of Jordan's hand and then pointed the women out of the room.

"That'll be all, ladies."

Twenty-Four

"**I**'ve had many ask me why I haven't accepted the fact that my twin is dead? I say to them people I have accepted the facts, and that's, my sister is still alive. You ask me how I know; the answer is— because I am her, and she is me. When she hurts, I feel her pain; when I'm sick, she's weak. It's always been that way. I know that my sister is still alive. She's out there somewhere. Just waiting to be rescued. London, if you hear me if you're watching me. Know this, I love you, and I always will." The words tumbled slowly and cautiously out of Paris's mouth, each one wrapped in a heavy voice.

They seemed to have echoed from the roof of her mouth, spreading their warmth everywhere. When she spoke, her words were clearer than Fiji water. She secretly prayed that her speech, her heavy southern accent, and sparkling eyes would send her someone to help find her missing sister.

"That was perfect, Paris. You did really good." Paris grabbed the Kleenex from Kimberly and wiped her running nose.

"You're going to be fine. I know this was hard for you, but I feel good about this. You definitely got the world's attention tonight." Kimberly's words comforted Paris, but she still cried like a baby. Paris had more than just London on her mind. She hadn't seen Kash, Stephanie, or baby Kash in weeks. She had selfishly blocked their numbers and didn't bother returning their calls after listening to their pleading voicemails.

"Paris, go home and get some rest. You need it, sweetie." Paris nodded in agreeance. She scooped up her purse and then her cell from the nearby table.

Expressing gratitude, Paris bid farewell to Kimberly as she departed from the hotel room Kimberly had arranged for the private interview with Good Morning America, saying, "Thank you, Kimberly, for everything."

"No, thank you. I know how hard this had to be, and I'm thankful for your time. You'll be amazed at how many women run from the fear of disappointment." Paris responded to Kimberly only with a smile, nodded her head, and finally disappeared through the door.

####

"I don't want to spend the rest of my life with you," Paris said to Kash as soon as he walked through the door. She was sitting on the loveseat in the living room. Two fried chickens, and wings, sat on a paper plate on the cocktail table. The salad was wilted, and the whole corn was soggy. Paris thought she could eat but failed miserably. Her appetite just wasn't worth a thing.

"How about, *Hey, husband. I miss you. Or Welcome home*?"

"Hey, Kash. How are you? But I meant what I just said, Kash.

"What is it now, Paris? What are you talking about?" He sat down on a stool at the counter with his long legs crossed at the ankle. The lace on one of his gym shoes was undone. The wife in Paris wanted to tell him about his shoelace, but then she realized that would mean creating some kind of intimacy, which was the last thing she wanted to do. She knew she needed to keep her distance because, of course, you don't stop loving someone in the blink of an eye.

Paris wanted to hate Kash, so she vowed to keep her focus on how pissed off she was and how hurt she felt. Falling apart would give Kash just the room he needed to touch her.

"What if I walked in here and said, *Paris, I don't want to spend the rest of my life with you*. How would you feel about that?" His words sent chills up Paris's spine.

"Is that how you feel, Kash?"

"Look, can I just get a glass of water and take a hot shower before you read me the riot act and tell me what I've done this time that's so deplorable? I'm beat, Paris."

"Take your time,"

Kash didn't look the least bit tired. In fact, he looked quite rested. *Maybe, he's been at one of his whore's house laid up*, Paris thought. He almost tripped over the shoestring when he pushed himself up to a standing position and took a step. Paris felt bad but not that bad.

"I see you got a new laptop," Kash said, staring at the new shiny red HP laptop on the kitchen table.

"Yelp," Paris answered, rolling her eyes.

"You like it?" he asked.

"They're all the same when you get right down to it."

"Were you able to recover all your stuff?"

"Yelp. You might want to look at yours after you get out of the shower." Paris said, propping her legs up on the sofa.

"Why did you try to use it?" *Oh, you have no idea*, Paris thought.

"I did, but I ran into some disturbing things," Paris snapped.

"What, did it have viruses too?" Kash stuttered suspiciously. Paris could see he was tempted to go into his office, but he was afraid to open the door. Paris felt he knew she had figured out what he did in his so-called office. Paris began to feel her stomach bubble up. The closer Kash got to the office, Paris became a little nervous. There was no doubt in her mind that there was no going back at this point. The situation was new to her; she had always been so obedient, and now, she was slowly becoming a nagging wife. She knew this wasn't how you end a marriage. She wondered deep down inside if she wanted to end it or just wanted to break up the boredom. She wished she could keep the parts of Kash she still loved. She wished she could pretend she didn't see the porn on Kash's computer or ignore the infidelity. Paris wished they still excited each other.

He turned down the hallway. Paris heard his office door open. Her heart was beating fast, and now she was anxious. She was tempted to lunge off the sofa, but for some reason, she didn't. She wanted to confront him from where she was sitting. She wanted him to stand still and look down at her, so his eyes couldn't avoid hers.

"Paris!" he yelled from the office.

"What the hell did you do with my computer, and where did you get all these damn pictures?" Out he came. He doesn't have the look Paris imagined. There's anger in his voice but not rage. After all, she had invaded his space. Violated his world, the one he thought was secret. Finally, after rambling through the pictures of him and his side piece that Paris had gotten from her private investigator, he rushed to the living room. Standing over Paris, just as she imagined he would.

"I had no idea you were such a freak," Paris said.

"I'm not a freak. What did you do to my computer?"

"What you think I did? I smashed it up with your hammer."

"You smashed it up?" he repeated.

"Did I stutter?" Paris replied. She stood up like a soldier.

"You're one sneaky, cheating, lying son-of-a-bitch, Kash, and I wished I'd down. I couldn't trust you from here to the corner!"

"You got shit all wrong!"

"How? There go the pictures with you and your whore; I saw the shit you watch on your laptop. I hate that I've given so much to you. All you've ever done was hurt me."

"That shit is old, Paris! You are tripping about nothing." Paris tried her best not to cry, but it felt like she was crying anyway. He took a few steps toward her, and she jumped back.

"Don't even think about fucking touching me."

"Paris, come on, now. Maybe I went too far with the porn, but I promise you, I haven't been with that girl. The pictures are old. None of this has anything to do with how I feel about you."

"Fuck you, Kash!"

"It's just something we do as a hobby."

"Who are *we*?"

"Guys!" He replied confidently.

"I don't care what guys do, Kash. How would you feel if you found a bunch of naked men on my laptop, huh? Or me out having a whole other life with a whole new man?"

"If you want to be a hoe, go ahead." Paris rolled her eyes at Kash. There was no hope for them, and that thought alone cut her heart deeply.

"Get out, Kash. Just go, please."

"Paris, this is not how you do a person you've loved most of your life." Paris didn't want to hear any of Kash's pleading because she knew that would only make her weak for him again. So, she began pushing him out through the front door.

"Paris, what are you doing?"

"Kash, you got to go; I can't do this anymore. It's over. There's nothing else left between us anymore. I'm tired of crying about you every night."

"Paris, I'm sorry, but can we at least talk about this?"

"There's nothing to talk about, Kash. I believe we will be better friends apart."

"Paris, you don't mean that."

"I do; now get out, Kash, please! Just do this one thing for me, please." Two more pushes, and Kash was out the front door.

Paris back slid down the door. It felt as if she was going down an elevator. Then it stopped. Her buttock slammed on the cold floor, and immediately, her heart began to ache. She could feel the thud. Then the acid tears ran down her face. The pain inside her chest felt like she was about to have a heart attack. She felt her elbows getting heavy, and she couldn't stop herself from kneeling over, so she went ahead and rolled into a knot but found herself rocking. She wanted to sit back up, but she just couldn't.

Paris looked around the house, and already, she could hear the silence. Her marriage was over. She would now live alone as a single woman. That thought broke her down, and she began sobbing until she was hoarse and sleepy, falling asleep where she sat. Flat on the floor, balled up like a baby in the womb.

Twenty-Five

"**I**'ve had many ask me why I haven't accepted the fact that my twin is dead? I say to them people I have accepted the facts, and that's, my sister is still alive. You ask me how I know, and the answer is—because I am her, and she is me. When she hurts, I feel her pain; when I'm sick, she's weak. It's always been that way. I know that my sister is still alive. She's out there somewhere. Just waiting to be rescued. London, if you hear me if you're watching me. Know this, I love you, and I always will."*

London's eyes were trained on some invisible ghost, her heavy eyelids a fraction too slow to blink, her irises too stationary. It was as if her brain was suffering a massive short circuit and was struggling to compute. Jordan moved into her line of sight and touched her cheek with the side of her thumb, and her lips formed a thoughtful grin. London's head tilted upward to Jordan's face, and her eyes slowly slid into focus.

"Come, baby, let us take you home." Omari and Jordan led London through the airport like she was a lost child. Some regulars who had spotted London on the TV from the picture started staring, whispering to one another. The only noise over their chatter was her repeating to Jordan and Omari, "She didn't give up on me. She didn't forget me." Over and over in a flat tone, her eyes bulk wide.

"Of course she didn't, baby." Jordan said.

"Omari, are you sure it's safe for us to be back in Atlanta?" Jordan asked as they boarded the UBER.

"Yes, Rasheed has been captured. It's safe for us to return."

####

The old painting leaned against the wall, dusty and unloved. London ran her finger along the gold framing, her pink nail polish almost purple in the half-light, and it came away dirty. There is now a streak of gold in the grime that must have taken years to form. She holds it up. With the light that struggles to make it through the grime on the window, the colors are subdued, but she can already tell it's an African scene. The hills roll green, intertwined with the golds of London.

London had it and many other paintings that she stole from Rasheed years back stashed away in storage that she had in Atlanta stuffed with many stolen items; expensive bags, diamonds, pearls, and designer dresses. London had been smart; she was constantly sending over her valuables with Rasheed's cargo. He had no idea about it.

He never paid attention to her missing things because he bought her so much. London got in good with one of Rasheed's workers, and every time Rasheed sent over a cargo full of girls or drugs, London had some of her things tucked away. Abdul, the worker, found her storage, and for a good fee, he kept the storage paid for, and in return, London kept food on the table for his family.

London had a bunch of homeless men and women she found on the street on her way to the storage to pack her U-Haul and her G-Wagon that she had shipped over as well. Thanks to Rasheed's hustle, it wasn't hard for her to do so. Rasheed sold everything; he was like Jay-Z; he could sell water to a well. On the boat of cars he had shipped to a dealership, London snuck her uncounted-for G-wagon on the boat.

The money wouldn't be a problem for London; thank God for Rasheed. She planned to sell the expensive paintings and pearls and maybe keep the diamonds for herself. Then take the money to start her own business and organization for missing girls.

"Be careful how you handle that," London said as the homeless guy packed the painting that was worth more than a million dollars.

"I gotcha, little momma. Trust me, I'll cut my hand off before I ruin one of these bad babies." London giggled at the guy's sense of humor.

"Naw, I don't need you to do that. You're going to need their helping hands."

"So, what side of town are you staying, Miss Lady?"

"It's not that far from here. Don't worry. I'm going to set you straight."

"Oh, I'm not in no rush, baby. That's fine." Instead of going to Stephanie's house like she dreamed for so many years, London decided to stay in a hotel. Just until she got her mind right. It had been well over five years since she saw her family, and she knew she couldn't just drop in on them. Plus, she was more nervous and scared to see them than she was ready to see them. She needed time to garnish up her courage.

Twenty-Six

"What do you mean you can't find Gunner anywhere? It can't be that hard to find an inmate."

"Stop yelling in my ear, Jordan. And hold on a minute. I'm at the grocery store." London pointed to the gluten-free honey-roasted turkey and nodded. "That's all," and then mouthing "Thank you" to the butcher.

"I've looked everywhere, I've looked him up on every prison site, and I can't find him anywhere. I even called a couple of prisons. I mean, it's like he doesn't even exist."

"Well, humans don't just vanish." Jordan thought about her statement right after it rolled off her tongue.

"Well, I kind of did," London replied.

"I didn't mean it like that, London. I'm sorry."

"What are you apologizing for?" London asked.

"It's just that it came out wrong." Jordan's whole tune changed.

"Chile, relax; I knew what you meant, and you're right, sort of. Humans don't just vanish. What if Rasheed has done something to Gunner?"

"How about you just wait until you talk to Paris. That way, you don't have to drive yourself crazy assuming things. I'm sure she can answer whatever you need her to answer." Silence erupts from the phone for ten long seconds.

"Hello?"

"I'm still here," London answered.

"I just don't think it's a good time right now."

"When is it ever going to be a good time. There is no good time." Again, London was hush mouth for at least twenty seconds this time.

"Stop stalling, London. Your family misses you, and you miss them. It is that simple, and everything that's complicated will be forgotten or worked out in due time. You've gone long enough without them. Don't you think you've suffered enough?" Tears formulate, but they don't drop. London stares around the store in a daze with her glistening hazel eyes.

"That's why I called you." Jordan said, pausing before telling her why.

"I'm listening," London said.

"Kash is throwing your sister a surprise party for her birthday, and I know you show up would be the icing on the cake. Talk about timing. I don't know a better time to reunite with your twin than on y'all birthday."

"Ok, fine. I'll go, but don't tell anyone, just in case I get cold feet and back out." Jordan's face lit up like a Christmas tree.

"Great! So, do you want to go shopping for clothes, big money?"

"Umm, I guess we can," London answered hesitantly. She couldn't focus on Jordan's conversation and her grocery list, so she just let Jordan talk. She had been standing in the frozen section for ten minutes in the same place, talking to Jordan, and she was freezing. It's cold as hell in the entire store, and all she had on was a white short sleeves t-shirt and some denim booty shorts. She tried to dodge the cold by pushing her cart down the can-good aisle, and what did she find, strolling down the aisle with a hyper kid in tow? Her very own twin sister.

"Mommy, mommy, can I get some fruit roll-ups too?" London's eyes and her mouth were frozen wide open in a stunned expression, and although she was staring straight at her son and twin sister, she appeared not to notice them. Quickly, she turned around and swiftly walked in the opposite direction of Paris and baby Kash.

"London! Are you there?" Jordan yelled into the phone.

"I'm not going to the party. I changed my mind. I believe they're better off without me." London said before she broke into sobbing.

"London, wait! What happened? What's wrong?" Without a response, London pushed the end button and zoomed out of the grocery store faster than a shoplifter. She didn't bother returning the groceries to their rightful place, nor the cart. She just had to flee the scene before she was made by Paris.

One call after another, Jordan wasn't giving up, but London wasn't giving in either; she sent Jordan to the voicemail each time. Her heart felt like it would jump out of her chest at any moment. Her only child was calling the only woman he knew as a momma, and she couldn't phantom the fact. Instant jealousy erupted through her soul, even though she understood the circumstances. How could she not? She figured if this was Karma, she had done a damn good job at paying her back.

The thought of interrupting the happily-ever-after didn't sit right with London. She didn't want to be a burden or mess up what Paris had going on. She had been enough problems already, sexing with her husband, then getting pregnant by him, and if that wasn't enough, she had to go off and get herself kidnapped, causing everyone to worry about her. The thoughts hunted London, and the more she thought about how much trouble her return could cause her whole family, the more she cried.

"By the grace of God, London made it back to her room. Her vision was blurry, and her nerves were shattered, but she made it back safely. As soon as she got into her private space, she broke down to her knees, calling out God's name loudly, pleading for him to guide her and heal her broken soul.

Twenty-Seven

Speechless, London stared at the small white stick. The pink plus sign confirmed her suspicions. She was pregnant. Mixed emotions filled her as her hands instinctively went to her flat belly. She turned to the side and lifted her shirt. She miraculously felt pregnant. All of a sudden, her nipples hurt. She felt bloated, and the nausea she had been feeling lately took a turn for the worse. Confirming it seemed to bring on all the symptoms at once.

London stared at herself in the bathroom mirror, and tears came to her eyes. She was joyful, unhappy, angry, and happy, all at the same time. She had a second chance at motherhood, only she was carrying Rasheed's baby. In her vision, she saw Rasheed little nappy-headed boy and or girl. Then she stepped back and peeked her head out the door to look at Hope sleeping face, and she was reminded, Rasheed genes weren't all that strong. Baby Hope was a curly-head baby doll.

In reality, she was pregnant by Rasheed, and although she hated him, she didn't have to hate their baby.

This could be a fresh start for me, London thought. Aborting a baby after God blessed her with it, even though she was occasionally taking birth control, seemed a little selfish. London had enough money to take care of her, baby Hope and the new baby. She had made a little over a half-million of the paintings she sold. She hadn't even got around to selling the expensive diamonds she had brought over from Africa.

I could just start over and let Paris and little Kash live in bliss, and I could be a good mother to baby Hope and the new baby. This could be my second chance at happiness, London thought. She chuckled at the thought. She would be a great mother, and her kids would be her everything. Paris and her could share parenting tips and leave the kids with Stephanie whenever they wanted to go out.

Now that two lives depended on her. She had no choice but to get things right with Paris and Kash. She instantly began to feel selfish as she thought of Rasheed. It was his baby too. Didn't he deserve to know that they had created a life together? *Nope,* she quickly concluded. God had perfect timing. London was overwhelmed with joy that she didn't have to raise her baby in Africa under Rasheed's supervision.

London: *Hey, Destiny, can you keep baby Hope for a couple of hours?*

Destiny: *Sure, London. Bring her on over.*

####

Kash and Paris held a special brunch at their home to announce the big news to all their loved ones. As they sat with a hand full of their close friends and family, Jordan, Omari, Nicole, Stephanie, and many others. They feasted on a catered buffet. Everyone was happy to see Paris and Kash looking so happy and carefree. Even Paris's best friend had begun to warm up to Kash. Initially, she was against Kash because she just felt like he was full of shit, but his action lately had proven he really loved Paris. It was love Nicole had grown to envy.

"I'd like everyone's attention, please," Kash announced as he stood to his feet.

"We'll like to thank everyone here for the role that you have played in our lives. Every person here has had an instrumental role in my or Paris's life, the reason for your invite today." All eyes were fixated on the happy couple as they stood at the head of the table holding hands.

"We are here to celebrate my baby Paris's birthday. We won't put her age on display. We all know how she feels about that." Kash joked as the party chimed in with laughter. While the party all laughed, London sneaked into the back of the room. She could see them, but they couldn't see her hiding behind the wall that blocked off the back porch from the kitchen.

"No, on a more serious note. Paris and I have decided to get a divorce." Instantly, the room became silent. You could hear a feather drop. London's heart dropped to her stomach; she, along with the other party guest, didn't see this coming.

"A divorce?" Nicole blurted out, finally breaking the silence.

"Yes, a divorce. We're ending our marriage but not our friendship." Paris added, looking Kash into his watery eyes.

"We mutually agreed that this was best for us." Kash didn't agree; if it was up to him, he would never divorce Paris. He was comfortable where he was, even if it wasn't perfect. Divorce was just something he didn't see himself having. He had always figured that he and Paris would be together forever, whether they were happy or not, just like his parents. They weren't always happy, but they made it work, and eventually, all the things that bothered them didn't bother them anymore. Kash badly wanted to say to their family friends, 'It was Paris's idea to get a divorce,' but he didn't want to be the one to start problems.

"We'll always love each other, and of course, we will continue to care for our son like two loving parents as we have always done." Paris's words stabbed London in her gut; hearing Paris call Kash her son was the worse feeling ever, but she understood it, and she wanted Paris to know that she would not cause any problems and that she was thankful Kash had someone to care for him like she did. Slowly, London eased around the wall. She was tired of hiding and was ready to face reality.

"We thank yaw for un..der..standing...." Paris's words got caught up in her throat as she stared her twin down. Tears dripped from her eyes, and the stunned expression pasted on her face was a dead giveaway that the energy in the room had changed. The party guest all turned around to

148

face the door where London stood. Everyone was speechless, all but Jordan, who jumped up from her seat to scream, "Surprise!"

London stepped from the shadows, stealing Paris's breath and the heat from her skin. Suddenly, Paris's defenses were just like paper - paper that was being soaked by the rapidly falling salty drops. Before she could draw in the air her body needed, she melted into London's arms. She inhaled Rihanna's *Crush* perfume and listened closely to her twin heart that beat as one with hers.

London's hands were folded around Paris's back as she drew her in closer. Both London and Paris could feel their body shake, crying for the missed time they will never get back, crying to release the tension of these five-plus long years. London pulled her head back and wiped Paris's tears with her index finger; her gentle touch brought more relief than Paris's heart could hold. When Paris kissed London on her blushed cheeks, it was the sweetest and most gentle, and it tasted of her tears. They wanted to speak, but all they could do was croak, "I miss you." "I miss you too, sister."

"Don't you ever leave me like that again!" London's mouth painted a soft smile, and then she nodded once before folding Paris in her arms again.

"Thank you for not giving up on me. You don't know how much that meant to me. I thought you didn't love me anymore!" London cried out on Paris's shoulders while the entire party watched with ugly faces and dripping tears.

"I would never give up on you, silly; you're my everything." Slowly, Stephanie walked up behind London as she and Paris hugged one another, rocking from one side to another.

"Can I get in on this love?" London knew that voice from anywhere; slowly, she turned around to face the only mother she knew.

"Momma! I miss you so much! I can't believe this is really happening. You don't know how many times I've dreamed of this moment."

"This is the best birthday ever!" Paris screamed out.

"How is this even possible right now? Like, where did you come from, London?" Proudly, London held out her arms towards Jordan waving her over towards her and Paris.

"This beautiful soul and her husband rescued me from the monster who held me captive in his world for over five years." Paris, Stephanie, and the rest of the party clapped as Jordan and Omari walked over to London.

"Oh, my goodness, Omari! You saved my sister?" Paris blurted out with tears continuing to scream down her cheeks.

"Oh, thank you, man." Kash pulled Omari in with one hand and patted him with another.

"You don't know how much this means to me and my family." Omari nodded his head with a large Kool-Aid smile on his face.

"No problem, man. I told you I was going to do everything in my power to bring her back. To be honest, I couldn't believe it was her. I couldn't believe that I had gotten so lucky to actually fall in her backyard out of all the land in Africa. When I laid my eyes on her, I knew I had to get her back to Paris. So, that's what I did."

"You definitely did, and I'm forever indebted to you and Jordan. I love you so much." Jordan couldn't speak; she was just lost for words. Tightly, she hugged London, and then finally, she murmured into her ear, "Life has been such a joy with you in it. I'm so glad God brought us together." The rest of the night was magical. The girls ate, danced, and reminisced on old times. The night was going so beautifully; the girls promised not to talk about anything too serious. They agreed it could wait, including the serious conversation that was bound to happen about baby Kash.

Twenty-Eight

Paris was on her way to meet London at a stable where Paris's horse, Cali, was stationed. Kash bought her the horse years ago when she found out he was cheating with the young chic from California, but because she had been so stressed, she barely rode the horse. As kids, Paris and London always wanted a horse, so Paris thought it would be cool if they took lessons together. The forecast called for a dry afternoon, and the wind felt lovely. It was a perfect day for London and Paris to finally sit down and catch up on everything, good and bad.

Stephanie had baby Kash in the car with her, and they followed behind Paris. For the first time, baby Kash was about to meet his real mother. Paris turned the volume up on the radio when she heard Mary Mary singing *Can't give up now*. Paris couldn't agree more. Three weeks ago, she had decided the only pill she was going to take was the antidepressant. She wanted to see how long she could go before feeling any withdrawal symptoms. And God must've been with her because, so far, she was doing good. Far better than she had imagined it to be.

In the past, the longest she had gone without Xanax was two days. She normally took one in a twenty-four-hour period, two tops, and the lowest dose. The only time she had trouble falling asleep was when she had a lot on her mind. Usually, Kash has issues or missing and thinking about

London. With Kash out of her life and London back in her life, she figured she should be good now.

She was done playing the game of hide- 'n'-go-seek with herself and from herself. Besides, the pills didn't make her feel any better the past was still the past. Nicole was able to tell she was on something, and Paris knew nothing good would come from that. Nicole would grill her every chance she got, and she couldn't blame her. She had lost patience with Paris. She was tired of feeling sorry for her, and Paris understood her frustrations.

Her cell phone started to vibrate, moved across the seat, and then failed on the floor. Paris couldn't reach it, so she pulled off the two-lane road onto the gravel shoulder. She put on her flashers and then reached to pick up the phone. It felt like something was suddenly spinning inside her head. "Shit," she takes a deep breath, exhaling quickly. It's London, she pressed TALK.

"Hey, London?" It's noisy in London's background; Paris takes the phone from her ear and stares at it as if she could see straight through it.

"London, are you at a bar?" Paris can hear glass clinking or something.

"Kind of," London replied.

"Are you drinking?"

"I've had a glass of wine. I tried waiting on you, but you were taking too long."

"I'm pulling into the parking lot, but I don't see your car."

"I'm at the clubhouse. It's the red building. I ordered you a glass of wine and momma sparkling water with lime. She's going to curse us out." London said, chuckling at her prank.

"She's definitely going to chop us to pieces. Her exact words going to be, *Now, how the hell I get water, and y'all get wine?*" Both girls burst into laughter.

Paris can see where London is from the car. She and Stephanie parked and walked in that direction, passing one beautiful horse after another, some being ridden, some being led. There are youngsters in cages practicing jumps. Kash is stunned; he can barely put one foot in front of the other from staring. Once they get inside, London is standing by a table close to the view of the horse with a baby attached to her hip. She looks stunning, with natural hair blowing in the wind, lip gloss popping, and her shape just flawless. Paris can barely wait to reach her so that she can ask, "Who is this?" She tickles baby Hope on the tummy and then gently pinch her cheeks.

"She's so beautiful," Stephanie added as she watched baby Hope giggle at Paris.

"This here is Hope Jackson," London said proudly with a smile reaching from one ear to another.

"Oh, my goodness, are you serious right now?" Paris blurted.

"As a heart attack," London replied before sitting back down in her chair.

"Oh my, we have so much to catch up on," Stephanie said as she took a seat at the table.

"So, who is this little fella?" London pinched baby Kash on the cheek.

"I'm Kash, and you must be my momma's twin because you look just like her?" Baby Kash's head turned from Paris to London, from London to Paris. He couldn't believe his eyes. His grandma had told him on the way over that they were about to meet Paris's twin sister, but he had no idea they would look so much alike.

"Yelp. That's my sister." Paris added as she took her seat at the table.

"So, how come I've never met you before." London's eyes glistened. She was staring her creation in the eyes.

"That's because I've been in Africa."

"You live in Africa?" Kash asked.

"Not anymore." London picked up her phone and quickly texted Paris.

London: *You don't have to tell him about me, Paris. I've been meaning to tell you this since I got back. I don't want to be a problem. I know he knows you as a momma, and I don't want to mess up anything.* London's feelings softened as she pressed send on her phone.

"Oh, I ordered yaw some drinks." London pushed over the glass of red wine toward Paris, a small cup of lemonade to baby Kash, and a glass of water with lime to Stephanie.

"*Now,* how *the hell I get water, and y'all get wine?*" Both girls burst into laughter. Stephanie said exactly what Paris said she would say.

"Are you ladies ready to order?" The thin brunette with green eyes came over to the table with a jolly spunky attitude.

"Yes, I'll have your grilled chicken salad with a side of chicken quesadilla." London wasted no time, she had been spying on the menu for a minute, and her mouth was watering.

"I'll have your steak and asparagus and glass of whatever they're drinking." London giggled some more.

"How would you like your steak, ma'am?"

"Well done," Stephanie said before taking a sip of London's wine.

"Hey!" London blurted.

"And you mine?" Paris stared down at her phone, reading London's text.

"Paris, do you know what you're having?" Stephanie said, hoping to get her attention.

"Well, you can give this little person your chicken tender kids meal," Stephanie said, ordering for baby Kash.

Paris: *I wouldn't dream of not telling him, London, you're his mother, and he should know the truth. What do you mean, you don't want to cause any trouble? You could never do that, sister. We're going to tell him exactly who you are. He doesn't have to move with you right away; we'll let him choose where he feels comfortable, but we're going to raise them, him and little Hope together. So, it really doesn't matter. I took care of him because he was my sister's son, not because he was my husband's son. Know that. Family over everything, always!"*

"Ma'am? Do you know what you're having?" The Caucasian waitress asked Paris for the second time.

"I'm sorry, yes, I'll have the same as her. A steak, well-done with the asparagus and loaded potatoes.

"Cool, I'll be right back with you ladies' order." London couldn't hold back her tears any longer before she could finish reading Paris's text; her tears began to drip.

"Are you okay?" Baby Kash asked London.

"Yes, baby, I'm good great." Before the ladies had noticed, hours passed. They talked about everything from baby Hope being Afia's biological daughter, to Paris's upcoming divorce, to Stephanie being cancer-free. They had so much to catch up on that they never got a chance to ride the horse.

"I just can't believe this, Gunner. I mean, thoughts of him are what kept me seem for so many years. And to think, this nigga is out here living like I never existed, and then with this Cardi bit...." London looked over at baby Kash and instantly filtered her words.

"He out here living up with this chic, like really, for real?"

"I couldn't believe it either, London. I was furious. He tried to convince me that he was looking for you, but he pissed me off because he wouldn't give Rasheed's name to the police." Paris said.

"Yelp, that's Gunner for you. Live and die by the G-code. But the nigga should have known he was going to need more help than he could ever garnish up himself when dealing with Rasheed. He knows how powerful this man is."

"Men and their pride, I tell you," Stephanie added.

"Exactly, you said. Men and their pride. He let his pride get in the way of saving me. I know he felt guilty, but he should have put all his pride to the side for my sake."

"Yeah, I know he felt guilty because he was responsible for your life being ruined. If I don't know anything else, I know he loved you. He just made some fucked up decision to me." Paris added.

"Yaw, also take a ride up there and surprise him," Stephanie said.

"You know what, that's a good idea." London was surprised to see Paris down for the cause. She had already made a mental note to take a trip to New York to find out some information on Gunner. But having Paris tag alone would be even better.

"Yeah, let's do that," London said.

"This should be fun," Paris said before she sipped more of her wine. She was on her third glass.

"I really just can't believe this is happening right now. I'm really back home with my family." London was also on her third glass of wine, and it had her emotions all over the place.

"Are you going to cry again, Mommy?" Baby Kash had warmed up to having two mothers quick. He thought it was the coolest thing ever.

"No, I'm not going to cry, silly rabbit." Kash burst into laughter as London tickled his stomach.

"This feels so good. I mean, I haven't been this happy in years. God has truly blessed us." Stephanie nodded her head in agreeance to Paris.

"Girls trip!" Paris blurted, holding her glass of wine up to meet London's.

"Let's do this," London said as their glass clinked together.

Twenty-Nine

A s soon as Paris and London stepped foot off the plane, they fell in love with New York all over again. The warm but cool weather, the hustle and bustle of the city, and the tall buildings made them feel like socialites. As they made their way through the airport, their beauty mesmerized the other patrons. They looked on as if they were someone famous, maybe from a reality show or maybe wives to someone famous.

London's aura exuded sexuality and beauty like no other. She was used to getting attention for her confidence, famous catwalks, and beautiful glow. Paris, on the other hand, was usually flaunting a good girl housewife look. She wasn't used to being called beautiful like London was. But London had given Paris a makeover, and she was glowing like Stella when she got her groove back. She was about to make New York her runway for the weekend. The girls made their way down the escalator, and the first face they saw in Egypt. In her hand, she held a sign that read, *have you seen my best friend London and her twin sister Paris?* She smiled brightly, genuinely happy to be reunited with her one true friend. After years apart and falling out like never before, it felt so good to have a chance to apologize. For years regretted not telling London sorry. She had believed for a long while she had missed her chance, thinking maybe London could be dead. That alone haunted her.

"London!" Egypt squealed as she and London embraced and swayed from one side to another.

"I'm so glad you're here!" London said with tears in her eyes.

"I'm so sorry, friend, for how I treated you. I should have never put that buster over you." Paris watched from the sideline with a huge smile pasted on her face. She was glad her idea didn't backfire. She knew how London could hold grudges.

"I couldn't wait to come, London. I was happy Paris invited me. I started jumping up and down when she called me with the good news. We miss you like crazy, chic. Now that we're back together, you can fill me in on your adventure." The girls skipped out of the airport like a group of high school chics.

"What hotel are you staying in?" Egypt asked.

"The Hilton. I got us a suite there. We're celebrating life this weekend, ladies, and there is no limit to the spending." With some of her diamonds now sold, London had money to blow. She was pushing over a million bucks, and she hadn't even sold all of her diamonds and pearls.

"Big shot!" Egypt said.

"Damn right. That was the only good to come out of being captured by a wealthy monster."

"Hell yeah, and we will cheer to that shit tonight, too," Paris added as they loaded the black SUV with their luggage.

"Hell yeah, it's a fuck nigga's get-money type of vibe tonight!" Egypt looked over to London and said, "Wait a minute. Paris got a man. A whole husband."

"Not no more, I don't." Paris blurted out before strapping her seat belt.

"What?" Egypt said.

"Yelp, you heard me right."

"But I thought yaw the perfect little couple?"

"Things are never what they seem, honey," Paris said, pursing her lips.

"Well, you haven't lied there. I have been single for years now." London turned her head to face Egypt.

"Say what?"

"You heard me right."

"So, I guess it really is, fuck nigga's tonight. Hey! We got to get Paris laid tonight, though, because I think she needs some good-good." London joked.

"Hell, I'm down for whatever." Both Egypt and London burst out into laughter. I couldn't believe little miss goodie-too-shoes was down to being trashy.

"Let's get this weekend started right!" Egypt sang out, and the twins co-signed by singing, "Hell yeeah!"

####

London, Paris, and Egypt were like movie stars as they wrecked Fifth Avenue, so beautiful that even women turned their heads with a mixture of jealousy and admiration as they strutted past. Stunning in Gucci, Channel, and Givenchy, the three women looked like they stepped off the cover of an Elle magazine. The girls were VIPs in all the stores. Champagne and caviar awaited them before they even stepped foot inside the doors.

London was in heaven. She couldn't believe she was back on her old stomping grounds with her sister and best friend. For years she dreamed of this day, but she really didn't believe it would happen. She had traveled the world with Rasheed, but it was like traveling with your overprotected daddy. Plus, he would take her anywhere but New York and Atlanta, her two favorite cities.

"So, I guess Paris has told you?" Egypt said with a serious tone.

"Are you speaking about Gunner?" London asked.

"Yeah, that buster!"

"Yeah, Paris told me a little, but I need to hear it from you in detail." London's heart dropped to her stomach dropped. She wasn't ready to hear the disturbing news, but she was all at the same time. The girls took a break from shopping to feed their bellies at a Burger and Lobster spot.

"This fool is running around town flaunting that thing Cardi on his arm like you, and she didn't get along. I mean, I could probably understand him moving on with a better option, but how the hell are you going to fuck with a girl you know London didn't fuck with?"

"Right, my thoughts exactly," London added.

"So, when I saw them together in a restaurant, I acted a fool on their ass. I was ready to beat that bitch ass and my date, a girl who I didn't even know from a can of paint. I'll tell you about that later, but he was ready to beat Gunner's ass, girl. He wasn't scared at all. Oh, plus, the ole boy who owned the restaurant wasn't hearing it either. I forget his name, but he was like *oh hell nawl Gunner, you got to go. How dare you bring that girl up in here? You know this was London's favorite spot.*"

London's heart smiled and frowned. She was happy to hear that people really missed her but sad to know that Gunner had been catching so much flack about her missing. She knew him like a book. He had probably been killing himself trying to find her, but Rasheed was just out of his reach. He prided himself on being a man, and she knew he must've felt less than her, knowing he was the reason she was missing in the first place.

"Have you talked to the creep?" Egypt asked.

"Nope, that's why we here because we about to pop up on that motha-fucka and get it cracking," Paris said, and London just couldn't believe the girl Paris had turned into.

"Well, aren't you just a gangster little thing now?" London joked, looking at Paris with a funny face.

"I'm just tired of these tired ass niggas, doing what they want and expecting us to just take it."

"Well, it's final then. We're going to show up on fuck boy Gunner's steps ready for whatever tomorrow." London listened as Egypt and Paris went back and forth about checking Gunner and about what they were going to do to him, and all London could think about was having a moment with him to herself. He was the love of her life, and she just wanted to talk to him alone. Touch him, feel him, maybe even have sex with him, depending on how he explained his behavior.

"Let's cheers to tomorrow!" Egypt said, raising up her margarita drink. Paris quickly raised her sex on the beach, then London hesitantly raised her rum and coke.

Thirty

BOOM...BAM... BOOM... BAM...BOOM...BAM!

"Who is it? London heard Cardi scream out.

"It's your neighbor; open up. It's important!" London had disguised her voice, sounding like a natural-born Latina. Paris held her hand over the peek whole, and as soon as Cardi opened the door, London swung on her, Brooklyn style. No questions asked.

Cardi didn't see it coming, but suddenly London's fist was slamming into her face while she sunk into her stomach. Blood pooled in Cardi's mouth as London banged on her. They stumbled apart for a brief second to catch their breaths before diving back at each other, eyes narrowed in determination. London dodged Cardi's fist and came up with her own; for a brief instant, her indigo-blue eyes widened before she managed to tilt her head back and slam it into London. Stars burst in London's vision, but she shook it off, blindly throwing a sloppy kick.

Cardi stepped back, easily evading the kick.

"Bitch, you don't come up in my house with that bullshit!" she crowed, smirking infuriatingly at London. London growled and then threw herself at Cardi, slamming onto the couch. London's blood hummed in her veins as determination and anger took over. One blow after another, she slammed her fist into Cardi's face.

"What the hell going on?" Gunner yelled out as he burst into the door.

"What you think is going?" Paris blurted out.

"What the hell are you doing in my house, Paris?" Gunner hadn't noticed London was the girl on top of Cardi until he aggressively pulled her off.

"Don't you ever put your hands on my fucking sister, bastard!" Paris had never punched anyone before, so she was incredibly surprised at the pain that blazed up from her arm as her fist connected with Gunner's jaw.

"What the fuck you do that for?" Gunner screamed out, holding his jaw.

"London?" Gunner and London, for the first time in over five years, locked eyes.

"You snake ass nigga!" There was something in that shout; it was pain behind it. Gunner watched. He watched London's eyes. Then he knew. The anger was nothing but a shield for pain, like a confronted soldier randomly throwing out grenades, scared for his life, lonely, desperate. He breathed in real slow. He knew his words had to be chosen wisely.

"Baby, I promise you, we'll need more than a couple of hours for me to explain to you everything." London knew Gunner's heart, and she trusted his words. He never did things without meaning. Her heart just wasn't convinced that he was the monster Egypt and Paris tried to paint him out to be. He and London had a special kind of love, a hood love neither Paris nor Egypt could understand. Egypt's first love was a buster, and Paris's husband was a professional square. They could never understand her and Gunner's union.

"What the fuck you mean, Baby?" Cardi yelled out.

"This bitch and her crew just barged into our home and fucking jumped me, and you calling this bitch baby?" Cardi lie came easy. It was as if she was telling the whole-hearted truth.

"Bitch! Didn't nobody jump you, hoe! London whooped your ass by herself." Egypt squealed out.

"Can yaw just give me and London a minute, damn! We need to talk, London, but we can't talk like this, baby. It's too many motha-fucka's running their mouths." London's eyes glistened as she stared blankly into Gunner's. She knew he was right, but she didn't have the courage to turn around and tell Paris and Egypt to leave.

"Who you calling a motha-fucka? You little pussy ass nigga!" Paris blurted out as Egypt yanked her back as she charged Gunner for a second time.

"London, can we please talk alone?" Gunner pleaded.

"So, you are choosing this bitch over me, Gunner, after all I've done for you?" Cardi snapped with her hands on her hip as she stood back on her left leg.

"London?" As Gunner called out for London's answer, her phone rang, temporarily saving her from the problem on hand.

"Hello?" She answered as she wandered off into the kitchen.

"Hey, can I speak to London?" Kenya said with a cracking, shivering voice.

"This is her; who's calling?"

"Hey, London, this is Kenya."

"Oh, hey, Kenya. You kind of caught me at a bad time. Can I call you back at this number?"

"No, you can't. I don't have long. This will only take a second." London finally noticed the stress in Kenya's tone.

"Is everything okay, Kenya?"

"No, it's not. I just killed Rasheed, and I'll probably be dead in a couple of days or hours; who knows, but that's not why I'm calling you." London could hear the hurry in Kenya's voice, so she didn't interrupt; she just listened.

"I'm listening, Kenya," London said as she plugged her right ear with her finger so that she could hear Kenya over all the bickering that was going on in her background.

"After I killed Rasheed, I took his phone and listened to all of his voicemails. The goal was to find where he was hiding my sister, but instead, I found who was behind your kidnapping." London's nerves rattled, and her guts bubbled like boiling grits.

"Go ahead, I'm listening," London said.

"It was that pussy nigga you love so much, Gunner. Rasheed promised to help him get out of jail if he gave him you. This nigga paid his debt off with you. He and Rasheed had been dealing with each other for years. Gunner thought Rasheed was going back on his deal because he didn't get him out of jail when he said he would, and that's when Gunner started leaving all kinds of voicemails on Rasheed's phone. He still has been doing business with him. He's even supposed to be sending Rasheed a Latina girl in the next couple of weeks." London looked over at Cardi; she was definitely Gunner's next meal ticket. She fitted the description to the tee. As much as she hated Cardi, she didn't wish that life on no one.

"I just wanted to tell you that, London, and I hope life is treating you well. And if I never hear from you again, just know I love you, and I'm very thankful for all you've done for me." Tears dripped from London's eyes slowly.

"I wish I could save you right now, Kenya." London managed to croak up with a lump in her throat.

"Don't you worry about me; God got me. Goodbye, London." Anger boiled deep in London's system, as hot as lava. It churned within, hungry for destruction, and she knew it was too much for her to handle. The pressure of this raging sea of anger would force her to say things she does not mean or to express thoughts she has suppressed for weeks. She knew she had to get out of everyone's way before she erupted in her furious state. She knew that this feeling would pass, but while it hasn't, she was well aware she could really hurt someone. So, she attempted to escape. Running towards the door.

But before she could make it, Gunner grabbed her by the arm.

"London, don't leave like this. We need to talk." He said.

"I would have never put it together," London replied calmly, with tears dripping from her face like a running faucet.

"Put what together, London?" Paris asked. She could see the pain painted onto London's face.

"You sold me to pay off your debt, you cowards ass nigga!" Before anyone could see it coming, London pulled out the 9-millimeter Glock she had just recently bought for protection and shot Gunner twice, once in the knee and once in the shoulder. Everyone in the house ducked, covering their heads.

"London, wait! Baby, wait!" He screamed out as he slid across the floor in his pool of blood.

"How could you, Gunner?" Tears were now dripping from Gunner's eyes. He knew he deserved everything London had in store for him.

"Go ahead, get over with, London. I can't even be mad at you. I deserve it." Cardi, Paris, and Egypt all watched suspiciously.

"Cardi, I don't hate you enough to let what happened to you happen to me. "Cardi looked at London's face as tears dripped from her hazel eyes.

"What are you talking about, London?"

"Tell her, Gunner!" London pointed the gun at Gunner's head.

"What are you talking about, London?"

"Don't fucking try me, Gunner. I will blast your ass." Paris began trembling; her heart pounded like African drums.

"He not worth it, London." Paris calmly said.

"Don't do it, London, please!" Egypt cried.

"What is she talking about, Gunner? Tell me now!"

"I don't know what she is talking about, Cardi; Damn!"

"Yes, he does! The bitch nigga was going to sell you to the same nigga he sold me to. Tell her the truth before I pop your ass, Gunner!"

"It was a set-up, London. I was trying to get you back. I just wanted to get the nigga in my possession so that I could get you back. I promise. I was only going to Africa to get you. It was all in my plan to get you. I promise, baby." Like never before, Gunner broke down into tears. Crying like a baby.

"He's not lying, London. I knew about him pretending to sell me, so we can find you. I was going to Africa of my own will." Cardi said. London rattling hand slowly eased the gun down from Gunner's head.

"You broke my heart, Gunner. You broke my heart, man. I loved you with all my heart, not just a little bit. Thoughts of you were the only thing that kept me sane all those years, and just to think, you were the reason I was over there. You were the only person who knew my location at all times. I should've known. It all makes sense now." Both Gunner and London's tears dripped from their eyes.

"I'm sorry, London. But trust me, I was never going to just leave you over there. It was just my only way out. They had shit over my head that couldn't beat with just a good lawyer. I needed that nigga connects, and I knew you were strong enough to handle yourself. What I didn't plan on. Is it taking so long for him to get me out? I figured I'll be out in a year or two tops and that I could trick the nigga like I was interested in business and get the fuck up out there. Trust and believe, I was going to rob the nigga blind. And I was coming to get you. I knew you were still alive, I just knew I couldn't tell nobody, or they fuck up everything." London shook her head with disgust as she slowly walked back towards the door.

"I can't believe you would do that to me, Gunner. How could you, Gunner?" London repeated until she was out the door.

"Come on, baby. You're going to be fine. I promise. We're going to get through this, London." Paris said as she wrapped her arms around her sister, leading her down to their rented car.

"His karma is greater than any punishment you could ever give," Egypt added as she followed behind.

"Don't you worry about shit; his guilt going to fuck him up alone," Paris said.

"I'm good. I'm better than I've ever been." London finally broke her silence to say before breaking down into sobbing.

The End!

If you'll like a spin-off starring Kenya, review and comment spin-off, please!

SEND PROOF ALL REVIEWS TO:

EMAIL – THEBOOKPLUG@YAHOO.COM

FOR A CHANCE TO WIN BIG IN A DRAWING. (ALL WINNERS ARE CONTACTED VIA MAIL)

➤ Autographed books

➤ Fly t-shirts

➤ Author swag bags

➤ Cool/exotic book marks

➤ Author swag mugs

➤ And very often, Amazon gift cards

Follow Author Cornelia Smith on Amazon